Broken

CW00457799

A story of hypocrisy, deception and corruption within the FBI.

Based on a true story. Names have been changed to protect the innocent and the guilty.

This book is dedicated to all those who have suffered at the hands of bullies in the work place.

Broken

Based on a true story.

"The best revenge is massive success" Frank Sinatra

Chapter One

Perplexed, Special Agent Jake Taylor hung up the phone. It was a dreary cold Friday night, the last day of January 1986. The last thing Jake expected was a phone call at his home from the owner of a local car wash. As a Special Agent, his phone number was unlisted? How did Mike Stein get his home number? What did Stein want to ask him, but couldn't ask him over the phone? Jake poured himself a large glass of B&B and tried to make sense of the call. Jake wasn't a friend of Stein, the only reason he used his car wash was because they were the only car wash he knew that would take the government credit card, and it was on his way home to his condo on Long Beach, Long Island, New York.

Special Agent Jake Taylor, an FBI agent (Federal Bureau of Investigation) from the New York office in Manhattan, was on a special detail to the Garden City INS office (Immigration and Naturalization Service) to assist in the backlog of Immigration problems. It was a welcome break from fighting the traffic to get to his office in Manhattan every day, yet Jake had a feeling that his life was about to get even more complicated.

Jake had started his career in the Justice Department following four years in the Navy where he served two tours in Vietnam. On the Kitty Hawk Aircraft Carrier, with the rank of an enlisted man, he had the task of a trouble shooter, the last person the pilot would see prior to their take off from the carrier. Not having ear protection from the noise of the high powered jets, by the time he had finished his four years, his hearing was irrevocably damaged. Upon his return to the States, he went home to Long Island, New York and attended college on the GI Bill, earning a degree in education. Jobs were scarce in the teaching profession at that time, however, a degree at that time could take you places. An advertisement for employment in the Justice Department appealed to Jake, he applied and after many background checks he took the position as a Special Agent in the Federal Bureau of Investigation. A prestigious position, which did not go unnoticed by his family. His mother would often boast about her only son and Jake wouldn't let her down.

Coming from a broken family, Jake had assumed the father figure for his mother and three female siblings at age 11. His father, a World War II prisoner of war, had been tortured by the Japanese in a prison camp and had come home a different man. His father was rarely around and in his depression had become an abusive alcoholic. Jake had witnessed terrible incidents between his mother and father when his father did show up. These incidents often lead to the young family, mother in tow, returning to their grandmother's home for safety. Jake was quite accustomed to sleeping under his grandmother's kitchen table. Jake was also accustomed to his father's belt. Although not together, Jake's mother would contact his father if Jake did anything wrong. His father always showed up to deliver justice.

After years of not knowing whether they would eat or not, Jake made it his responsibility to take care of the family. Although his mother worked as a waitress, sometimes the money would only cover the rent. Sometimes it didn't, which usually meant a change of address. He worked every job he could. If his wage wasn't enough to provide food, he would steal apples from a tree and bring them home to his family. He grew up very quickly and missed the whole childhood part. He told his school friends that he lived in a large house in Westbury, when in actual fact he lived in a one bedroom apartment at the rear of the big house, with all his siblings. It took him many years after he finally retired to own up to that one! Every weekend, during the school year, he would take his old bike and ride to the other end of town, to a laundromat. He was too embarrassed to wash his school clothes in the local laundromat in case anyone would see him. Often times he would not have enough money to dry his clothes so, Monday morning, he would get up early and use the iron to take any dampness out.

When he finally hit graduation, not even 18, he signed up with the military, not for God and Country, but because "that's what poor kids did'. Within 48 hours at Navy boot camp at Great Lakes Recruit Training Command, he was promoted to Recruit Petty Officer in Charge of 76 men, some of whom were college graduates four years his senior. He sent every pay check home to his mother together with audio tapes explaining what was happening with him and asking for details on what was happening State side. He had left his first girlfriend Michele back home in Long Island where they had each promised to wait for each other. She gave him a St Christopher medal to protect him while he travelled abroad. Two years later he received a "Dear John" letter from Michele saying she had found new love. When we returned from Vietnam and back to the lifeguard chair, he attached the medal to his lifeguard whistle. One of the young female lifeguards spotted it and asked its meaning. Jake explained its significance and told her that Michele had sent him his "Dear John" letter while serving in Vietnam.

"Wow" she exclaimed, "we all thought your name was Jake".

Jake's father died at age 50 of a failed liver. When Jake discovered his body in a small apartment next to a cheap bottle of wine, he found all the letters which Jake had written to him from his time in the Navy. Although his father had never once told Jake that he was proud of him, Jake hoped that he had kept his letters because secretly he was.

Jake attended the Federal Law Enforcement Training Academy in Glynco, Georgia. Once graduated, he started his work in the FBI in Manhattan. Eager to fit in, he got involved with a group of agents who would frequently bet on various sport events. It didn't take long until Jake was completed enmeshed in gambling and had a bookie to whom he owed a good amount of money. It seemed that everyday there was a different sporting event to bet on. When the US was out of sports to bet on, then Canadian sports were used. Jake was on an emotional dollar coaster, never winning enough to pay off the bookie. This lead to more betting and a daily vicious circle. His fellow agents seemed to shrug off their losses confident that they would win the next one. Jake would stress about each loss and found himself unable to sleep at night as he tried to plan his exit from gambling. One morning, after a difficult night, he read in the newspaper about a local realtor who had got involved in gambling. He had been arrested and was now going to prison after stealing from the escrow accounts from his realty customers. This story really struck to the core of Jake. While he was working on an DEA task force, Jake could seize thousands of dollars in cash at a time. Fear gripped him as he wondered, in desperation, if he was capable of stealing DEA money to pay his debts?

That night he had a nightmare where he had stolen some money from a crime scene. He had placed the money in a brief case and then into his personal car. As he tried to leave the scene, a sniffer dog had alerted its handler to Jake's trunk. It was this nightmare that forced him to do one more big gamble to see if he could pay off all his debts. He bet every dollar to his name on a horse which he had researched extensively. As the horse ran, Jake could not watch and spent the race in the restroom vomiting. He must have had an angel on his shoulder that day. His horse won. Jake was able to break even with his bookie and walk away. He never gambled again!

That night Jake lay in bed trying to guess what Stein was going to ask him. Why had he called him at home? How did he get his number? As he fell into a troubled sleep,

"Just say No" kept repeating itself in his head. A picture of Nancy Reagan sat on her horse touting a large sign "Just say No to drugs" was enough to wake him up.

"Jesus, I'm never going to drink B&B again".

The following morning, Jake switched on the TV while he sipped his first cup of coffee. The television was broadcasting the memorial ceremony for the seven heroes lost in the challenger shuttle explosion. Images of President Reagan filled the screen as he played tribute to their brave sacrifice. Haiti was declared to be in the state of siege following antigovernment demonstrations. There was talk of Nelson Mandela to be freed and the first artificial heart was implanted in a woman in Minneapolis.

As Jake watched, none of the news registered with him, his mind solely revolving around the phone call last night. Annoyed, Jake flipped the television off, dressed quickly, a pair of jeans, sweatshirt, ball cap over his tousled blonde hair and sunglasses hiding his crystal blue eyes. With renewed effort in his step, he started his car in the condo parking lot, threw it in gear and headed to Valley Stream and to the East Side Car Wash.

Stein's wife, Diana, looked up from the magazine she was reading as she stood behind the counter, inside the car wash lobby. She greeted Jake and ushered him into the back office. Stein sat at his desk and jumped to his feet as Jake entered the small dark cluttered room.

"I had a feeling you would come Special Agent Taylor" Stein declared and beckoned Jake to sit in the chair opposite.

"This must be important for you to call me at home" Jake replied, continuing to stand.

Slowly, Stein stood up from his chair and looked directly at Jake

"I have a feeling that you may be able to help me with a problem I have"

Jake pondered a moment before sitting down in the chair opposite Stein's desk. He leaned back and waited for him to continue. Stein sat on the edge of the desk grinning,

"I think I have a way that you and I can make some serious money"

Jake continued to sit motionless as Stein continued.

"I know of an individual who needs help with the immigration process"

Stein paused as if to wait for a reaction from Jake. He received nothing so he continued,

"In fact I know of five people willing to pay $10,000 each to get their permanent residency cards, you know, their green cards"

Jake, although without facial expression, was experiencing a cascade of emotions, anger, disbelief and shock, to mention a few.

Slowly Jake stood up from his chair, walked to the office door, without looking at Stein he left the office.
 "I'll think about it"

Jake had no intention of thinking about it!

The lobby at Victor's was packed as Jake ushered his mother through the front entrance. Victor, in his deep Italian brogue, came running toward mother and son, his arms waving in the air.

"Bongiorno Bongiorno this way Señora, Señor. I have the perfect table"

As the Sunday church crowd at the bar turned to see which royalty had just skipped the line, they were afforded the view of an elderly lady and her son being seated at the best table in the house.

Waitresses stopped what they were doing, brought bread rolls and Jake's favorite wine to the table, all the time Victor was cleverly orchestrating the dance while shouting,

"Prego Prego Andiamo"

Jake's mother loved the attention. She beamed and graciously nodded as her wine glass was filled and "usual" order taken. She had often told her friends of the privileges her son was afforded being in the FBI. Little did she know that the privilege was driven by Victor's fear of what Jake could discover about his establishment if ever chose to look.

"So Mom, what did you think of Father McMurray's homily today?"

"The man is impossible to understand with that thick Irish brogue"

"So similar to your mothers thick Irish brogue" Jake retorted.

His mother did not even look up from sipping her soup.

"He was referring to the "Golden Rule" Mom.

"Why didn't he just say that? No, it took him 22 minutes; 22 long long minutes. He is insufferable. I much prefer Father Henry. His homilies are short and to the point"

Jake thought about telling his mother how she could also be insufferable at times, but decided against it.

With his Mom safely back home in her apartment in Westbury, Jake drove slowly through the dirty brown slush to his condo. The streets were quiet and it was almost dark by the time he had parked the car.

As the wind howled and rattled the glass of his large condo windows, Jake looked out upon the dark raging ocean highlighted by a full moon. Even the seagulls were absent, huddled up together somewhere trying to escape the bitter cold.

Jake drew the curtains and called his buddy Rick, a fellow agent. Rick listened as Jake recounted his incident at the car wash.

"Shit Jake, how do you do it? Just when I thought you were out of the frying pan, you get right back into the fire. I don't know what to tell you man except to lie low"

In 1984, Jake was sworn into a special division of the US Customs service, detailed to Nancy Reagan's "Just say No" fight against illegal drugs. This prestigious promotion had been bestowed on Jake after years of exemplary service on the streets of New York City. Jake was ecstatic at the promotion, and to show his appreciation, he wrote to the Commissioner of Customs, William von Rabb, thanking him for the opportunity. Jake was even more amazed to receive a reply from the Commissioner in which he commended Jake for his many successes and expected Jake to do well within US Customs.

This promotion did not sit well with Special Agent Dave Valerio. Jake was everything that Dave wanted to be. Jake was a good-looking man, popular with the guys and the women. It seemed every time Dave saw him out in public, he was with a group of different people and having a great time. Dave was stuck in a loveless marriage and had recently been assigned to the Office of Professional Responsibility for the New York area. This was a particularly despised office as the investigations were internal and targeted the officers themselves. The agents working for OPR were ostracized and mistrusted.

The evening of the "swearing in" ceremony for Jake Taylor, an impromptu celebration was held at the Poets Corner pub in Manhattan. Agent Dave Valerio happened to be sat at the bar at the same pub, complaining to his brother-in-law about his wife and his miserable life.

Jake and the gang boisterously entered the bar laughing and shouting. They positioned themselves close to where Dave and his brother-in-law sat at the bar. Rick saw Dave and called him to come over and join the party.

"This is how it should be done Dave" Rick quipped. "Come take a lesson from Jake"

Furious, Dave stood up, slammed his drink onto the bar and walked out.

"What's up with him" Jake yelled across the bar.

"Life" Rick blurted out and collapsed, laughing, into a bar chair.

From that day, Special Agent Dave Valerio made the downfall of Jake Taylor, the sole purpose of his existence. He would indeed take a "lesson" from Jake.

After hanging up with Rick, Jake poured himself a drink and slumped into his beaten up, extremely comfy lazy boy. How the hell did he end up back in the fire, as Rick has so delicately put it?

It was almost a year and a half since Jake had been sworn in, together with twenty-four men and women, as a Special Agent in the US Customs Service. The other 24 had already assumed their positions within the service, men and women without Jake's credentials; a decorated war Veteran, a college Grad with honors and an impeccable reputation.

It became obvious to Jake that something else was going on. After countless phone calls to supervisors and office management, he filed a Freedom of

Information Act request. Two months later was stunned to discover that he was under investigation by the Office of Professional Responsibility namely Agent Dave Valerio.

Jake closed his eyes and decided to take Rick's advice and "lay low". He would call Mike Stein the following morning and decline his offer.

At 2 a.m., Jake sat bolt upright in his bed.

"Shit, it's an integrity test"

At times, Agents would be given phony information to see if they would do "the right thing" and file a report.

Jake shot out of bed. This whole thing reeked of Valerio. For the next hour, Jake put pen to paper and documented everything that had happened over the phone on Friday night and at the car wash on Saturday.

Jake was the first one in the Garden City Office on Monday morning. He showed his statement to Special Agent Fred Lemar, as he walked through the office door, coffee in hand. Special Agent Lemar faxed the document immediately to the Manhattan office.

Agent Lemar asked Jake if he could accompany to his office. Jake sat at his desk while Fred Lemar explained that Manhattan FBI wanted a polygraph on Jake before he officially started work. Jake rolled his eyes. This was definitely not standard practice and he knew that Valerio was behind this request. Jake had nothing to lose and everything to gain, so Jake signed the consent form. The questions that were asked, progressively became more focused upon personal acts of corruption against the Justice Department. Suddenly, Agent Lemar stood up and advised Jake that he would have to leave the room for a moment. This was a well-known tactic in investigations. Agent Lemar had left his notes on his desk. Underlined was the statement "Possible renegade and corrupt agent."

Jake read the notes and sat back down stunned at what he had just read. His integrity was been held in question, yet, by using this tactic, Agent Lemar had indicated to Jake that he trusted him.

It soon became quite clear that the Stein situation was not an integrity test. Jake was called into his supervisor's office late morning. Ted Caturo, a twenty year veteran of the agency, had a broad grin across his rugged face.

"Agent Taylor. It seems that you are quite the charmer. We have been watching Mike Stein for some time and now we have a way in. You! Welcome to code name Adonis"

Under his breath Jake muttered,

"Jesus, Manhattan already thinks I'm a dirty Agent, I should be good at this"

Ted asked Jake to join the team for lunch. They were heading to a local cafe. Ted told Jake to ride with him so he could fill him in with more details about Adonis.

In the garage, Ted popped the trunk of his government vehicle. Within the trunk was a child's playpen and toys, a clear violation of the rules. This was another huge indication of trust for Jake. Ted had just exposed his vulnerability and at the same time indicated that he believed Jake was not a corrupt agent. Ted Caturo, seven years later became the Special Agent in Charge (SAC) of the New York FBI office, a very prestigious position. Upon his retirement, he went into business with former Mayor Rudy Gulliani and continued to work for the betterment of New York City.

Chapter Two

"Mike Stein please"

Jake on a recorded line waited for Stein to pick up.

"Yeah"

"Is this Mike Stein"?

"Who wants to know"?

"Special Agent Taylor"

"Hey what's up Special Agent Jake Taylor"?

"I've thought about your proposition. I'm in on one condition. I set the rules"

"Sure thing Jake. Your rules. I guess that makes us partners"

"Hell no, I'll be in touch" Jake hung up the phone with a sick feeling in the pit of his stomach.

It was another frigidly cold morning as Mike Stein and Jake walked along Sunrise Highway. Long range cameras clicked in a car tucked away in a parking lot as back up agents Lemar and Sands photographically documented the meeting.

Jake was wearing a wire and his voice crackled over the transmitter in the back up agent's car.

"Stein, this isn't going to happen overnight. It has to look right. It's going to take at least two months to get permanent residency status so we can go through the proper channels"

"Man, they ain't gonna be happy!"

"Listen this is my career on the line. If we do this, it's got to look right"

"Yeah, I'd promised them a couple of weeks"

"Stop making promises I can't keep. I need to meet these guys. I need passports, photographs and paperwork filled out; I also need $2000 up front".

"I told them $1000"

"My rules Stein, set it up, public place"

Jake walked away. He still had that sinking feeling in the pit of his stomach. He reached the car and headed to a Greek diner. He headed straight to the restrooms.

Back in the Garden City office, Lemar and Sands met him with silly grins on their faces.

"What's the joke" Jake asked

"You may want to turn off the transmitter when you use the bathroom"

The following day, Jake heard from Stein and one of "his clients" needing the permanent residency status, Lorenzo Endario. Jake said he would call them back momentarily and did so from a recorded line.

"Jake, I have Lorenzo with me. Tell him what he needs to bring to the meet"

"You will need your passports with the I-94 entry form, photos and the paperwork completed which I left with Stein. I can get you a temporary residency stamp in about a week. The permanent will take longer. I also need $2000 upfront in cash, large bills. There is a diner in the Rockville Centre called the Four Way Stop. I will meet you there, this coming Monday at 2pm"

"I will bring Lorenzo as well as Jusieppi D'Abrevio to the meet."

"Don't be late, I won't have much time".

Plans were made for Agents Lemar and Sands to be back up. They would be in the diner taking photos and Jake would wear a wire.

That weekend, before the meet, Jake had an uncomfortable feeling that things were maybe going too well. On Saturday night he met up with Janice, his friend for many years. Janice had got him through some of the worse times in his life. They had met in college after Jakes' four years with the Navy was up. They had remained friends for years. Janice complained to Jake when things were going wrong in her life, and Jake did the same. Janice was the ultimate sounding board and the advice she gave always worked out. Jake hoped his advice was the same, but never quite knew.

He confided in Janice often, this time no different. As they sat and shared a bottle of wine, Jake talked about his fears with Adonis. Janice remained silent as he relayed his discomfort in the fact that all was going too well.

"Jeez Jake, I would be happy that things are going well. Play by the rules and watch your back"

It was another miserable Long Island day that following Monday. It was March 21st, 1986 Jake's mother's birthday. Snow had turned into rain which had then frozen leading to accidents up and down the highways. By the afternoon, the ice was melting and so Jake decided to go ahead with the meet. Agent Lemar helped Jake put on his wire,

"Testing, testing" Jake repeated over and over again!

"Try it again Jake" Agent Lemar yelled from the other side of the office.

"Testing, testing, testing, shit this thing is not cooperating"

There was no time for another wire to be placed. Agents Lemar and Sands needed to leave to get to the diner before the others arrived. Jake pulled off the wire. Frustrated, Jake told the agents that he would write a report once he got back to the office.

He arrived at the diner and saw Agent Sands at a corner table. He thought he saw Lemar behind the counter but was not sure. Stein, Lorenzo and Jusieppi were sat in a large booth about half way across the room. Stein jumped up and introduced everyone before Jake had even made it to the table. Jusieppi was a weasley looking man with pointy features and slick black hair. Lorenzo, on the other hand was a bear. Big, tall with hair down to his shoulders and very unshaven. Jake nodded in Lorenzo's direction and was about to sit down. Lorenzo had other ideas. He grabbed Jake in a bear hug and discreetly patted him down. Thank God the wire had malfunctioned Jake thought at the same time as muttering to Lorenzo,

"What the hell are you doing? Do that again and you don't walk out of here"

Stein pushed Lorenzo down into the booth, with gritted teeth and looking directly at Lorenzo, he muttered,

"He won't, believe me."

Still shuck up, Jake maintained his composure and took the passports and paperwork handed to him from Stein. Lorenzo and Jusieppi, at Stein's signal, stood up and left the diner.

Stein handed Jake an envelope containing the $2000 they had agreed upon. Jake was about to get up and leave but Stein reached across the booth and put his hand on Jakes arm,

"I have some other business we have to talk about"

Jake brushed Stein's hand off his arm and fired a threatening look at him. Stein raised his hands in the air,

"I'm sorry, I'm sorry. Jeez you need to relax Jake" Stein blurted out.

"What" Jake demanded?

"I'm involved in some other business that you may be interested in. That Mercedes outside was not bought with car wash money"

Jake relaxed back in his seat and beckoned for Stein to continue.

"I dabble in the drug business, mainly cocaine. I can get as much as I like" Stein boasted and went on:

"I have a supplier, Bob Branson. He's one of the big guys, owns the Six Towns Car Wash in Florence NY. Bob buys around $100,000 worth of kilos and distributes it. I've known him for years. Are you interested?"

"Yeah I'm interested, but I need a sample first" Jake tried to look cool and nonchalant, inside his stomach was doing flips. "Just cocaine, or does he have other product?"

"Now now Jake, don't get ahead of yourself. Yeah, he has qualudes and some other stuff, but the money's in the coke"

"Shit" Jake answered, "You know your stuff!"

Stein loved to talk big and took the bait.

"I've been doing this for years" he boasted, "I have another buddy who has a chop shop in Brooklyn. You need a car to disappear, $500 and it's gone. The body shop up the road calls me for parts, I supply. I just made a quick grand on a part for a 1980 Corvette. Supply and demand man! I have the supply and I am in demand" Stein laughed at his own joke.

"I'll have your sample by the end of the week" Stein said as he rose from the booth. He threw a ten dollar note on the table and then walked out of the diner.

Jake followed a few moments later, his head spinning. He drove back to the office quickly and knocked on Ted Caturo's door.

"Boss, this thing just got real big real quickly"

Jake explained what had just transpired and that he wasn't wearing a wire. Ted told him to write everything up and have it on his desk within an hour. In the meantime, he would get DEA involved.

As Jake sat as his desk, transcribing the events of the afternoon, the phone rang. It was Mike Stein. Jake quickly told him that it was difficult for him to talk and that he would call him right back from a different location. He alerted his supervisor Caturo and Agents Lemar and Sands. They all listened as Jake placed the call on a recorded line. A female answered, obviously chewing gum. She shouted for Stein to pick up.

"Yeah" Stein answered.

"It's Jake"

"Yeah, about that matter we discussed, I should have something for you to pick up next week, no problem. Also, I have a couple of Israeli customers who would like Special Agent Jake Taylor to get them Permanent Residency cards. They would need visas for their families also. I negotiated $14k on your behalf"

"I'll meet you next Thursday at the car wash at 3pm to pick up passports and anything else you might have for me " Jake replied and hung up.

Supervisor Caturo scratched his head and told Jake that there was not enough time to get DEA on board in time for the meeting with Stein on Thursday afternoon. Jake would wear a working wire, have back up, but he would have to continue to go it alone. In fact, Jake preferred it that way. His rules!

The sun finally broke through the clouds on the Thursday meeting day. Jake was tired having downed a bottle of wine the night before at his mother's apartment to celebrate her birthday. It seemed that wine was the only way he was guaranteed a decent night's sleep these days.

The office was quiet when he arrived, coffee in hand. He immediately went to the wire room; he was taking no chances this time and would find a wire system which worked. With Lemar and Sands as back up, Jake made the familiar journey to the car wash.

In the back office, Stein was leaning back on his office chair with his feet propped up on the desk. As Jake entered the dimly lit room, Stein nodded his head and smiled.

"My man, Jake, sit down" he beckoned to the only other chair in the office next to a small file desk.

Jake sat. Stein pointed at the file cabinet next to Jake.

"Open that top drawer and see what awaits you" Stein drawled with a creepy grin on his face.

Jake opened the drawer and found a small vial containing about a gram of white powder.

"Try it man, tell me that it's not the best you have ever had" Stein continued, now standing behind his desk.

Immediately Jake stood up,

"If you want this relationship to last, you do not want me testing the goods. Shit, I would fail a pee test and that would be both me and you done. No I'll take it to my buyer"

"Jesus, I never even thought of that. Christ we would be done for" Stein replied. "We are dealing with the big boys here. Yeah, the really big boys. This is top shelf stuff. We could find ourselves in a fucking dumpster with no problem. Even under the fucking dumpster. Our big boy has big friends. Big loyal friends. Jesus, I got to be so careful these days. I gave my hairdresser Fred a gram of coke for Christmas as a tip. The next day, a customer of Fred, a fucking lawyer, comes into the car wash wanting to buy cocaine."

Jake sat back down. He didn't want to rattle Stein anymore.

"Don't panic, we got this. We are going to make this happen. Watch your back and I'll take care of mine. Now what about these Israelis?"

Stein, reached into his safe at the side of his desk and gave Jake $1000 in cash and four Israeli passports.

"You see, this is a good relationship. We both have something the other one needs. I have the coke, you the green cards. A mutually profitable relationship"

Back at the Garden City office, the $1000 cash and the vial of "white powder" were taken into evidence along with copies of the passports. The following day, the powder was taken out of evidence and transported to the Drug Enforcement Administration (DEA) laboratory on 57th in Manhattan where it was weighed and analyzed. The results: 95% pure cocaine.

With DEA now in the picture, Jake set up a meeting with Stein away from the car wash so photographs could be obtained by back up agents Lemar and

Sands. The meet was at Lister Field close to Rockville Centre, Long Island. Jake, wearing a wire, pulled his government car into the parking lot at Lister Field. He immediately noticed two unmarked police cars in the lot. He pulled out of the parking lot when he noticed Stein in a late model BMW. He motioned to Stein to follow him and pulled over in a more secluded area. Jake got out of his car and got into the BMW.

"You see the unmarked cops in the lot" Stein immediately questioned.

Jake nodded changing the subject,

"Nice car, new?"

"Yeah, it's the wife. Can never make up her mind what she wants; first it's a Merc, now BMW. Happy wife, happy life"

"I hear you" nodded Jake. "I checked out the quality of the coke you gave me. Very satisfactory my friend!"

"How much do you need? Larger quantities, better price!"

"I want you to meet my friend Tania. She will be doing most of the buying for her clients in the Hamptons. I'll have her drop in at the car wash next week and you can meet her. She is willing to pay $2000 cash for an ounce of Cocaine. Once her clients approve, she will be buying in larger quantities".

Stein looked uncomfortable. I want to deal with you Jake, no one else. I don't know if this broad is a cop"

"If she is then I'm in trouble. Come on Mike. I got to look legit. I can't be coming to the car wash every week. It will look suspicious. Tania is clean. She's a friend"

"I'll think about it", Stein muttered. "We never agreed to this".

Jake quickly interjected,

"On another subject, I need to see Lorenzo and Jusieppi. I need their fingerprints and new photos for their Alien Registration cards. I have their passports with temporary alien registrations and employment authorization impression stamps. I can meet them at the diner next Friday around 11am. You don't have to be there but no more shit from Lorenzo or he's done"

Stein nodded as Jake exited the BMW. He pulled away from the curb spinning his wheels and creating a squealing noise. Way to stay unnoticed, Jake thought as he got back into his government car.

Back at the office, Special Agent Tania Rowen from DEA was talking to Ted Caturra, Jake's supervisor. Tania and Jake had worked together before in a sting operation some years back. Tania followed Jake to his office and over a cup of coffee, they caught up, laughing at some of the encounters they had seen during their past operations, then getting more serious as Jake filled her in on Adonis. He told Tania about how nervous Stein was at getting caught and how important it was for her to boost Stein's ego when she did get to meet him. This was the only way she would ever earn his trust.

Jake and Tania left the office together and stopped in at a local bar for a drink. Tania questioned Jake about his run in with Agent Dave Valerio. Jake told her that he believed that his detail to the Garden City Office was to keep him out of the way. Tania told Jake that Valerio was well known to the New York DEA office. She also told him that he wasn't the first person Valerio had tried to ruin. The last guy being indicted. She indicated that Valerio was the most despised Agent in the office, but he had power. Most Agents were frightened of him because they saw what he did with those who did not comply with his orders. The further Jake was away from Valerio, the better he would do.

They left the bar around nine and arranged to meet the next morning at the office at 8am so Tania could listen to all the tapes Jake had made while working with Stein.

"It's going to take time to get you in with Stein. He likes me, trusts me, he's just real scared. Bob Branson is linked with organized crime. He's one of the big boys. His son has done time already. Stein has seen what he has done to other talkers. I guess they are not talking anymore. Branson owns Six Towns Car Wash in Florence, NY. Everything is cash only. We believe the car wash is the front for money laundering for his drug business. Seems Branson has clients in Manhattan, Brooklyn and Queens. Stein thinks he is the only dealer in Long Island, I know for a fact he is wrong".

It was another miserable, wet day on October 21st, 1986 as Jake, with back up from Sands and Lemar, entered the Greek Four Way Stop diner. Lorenzo and Jusieppi were sat at a round table in a booth towards the back of the restaurant.

"Good morning Gentlemen" Jake spoke as he shuffled into the booth. "I trust you have four passport size photographs each for me. I will take your fingerprints and then we will be done"

Lorenzo handed over both sets of photos sheepishly and began to say,

"Special Agent Taylor, about last time…."

"No need, let's get on with it"

Within ten minutes, Jake exited the diner and drove to the Immigration and Naturalization Service (INS) Office at the Federal Building in Manhattan and handed them to the Agent in charge in conjunction with the ongoing investigation.

By early December, Jake had finally convinced Stein to meet Tania. Tania met up with Jake at the Garden City office on December 23rd, 1986 and they drove together to the EastSide Car Wash in Jake's government car. Back up parked across the street from the car wash. Both Tania and Jake wore a wire.

"Ready" he questioned Tania

"As I'll ever be" Tania retorted as she slammed the car door and followed Jake into the lobby area. Stein was waiting for them and ushered into the small, dimly lit back office.

"Mike, meet Tania"

Without waiting for a reply, Tania reached out her hand,

"Mr Stein, I've heard such good things about you. I can't wait for us to work together. Let's make some money"

Stein, obviously uneasy, without shaking Tania's hand, looked at Jake and pointed to the file cabinet in the corner of the office.

"Your product is in the top drawer"

Jake pulled out a brown paper bag, and carefully opening it, found a clear plastic bag inside containing white powder. He passed it to Tania. Tania passed a wad of $20 notes to Stein,

"If it's as good as Jake tells me it is, I will be wanting larger quantities."

Still looking at Jake, Stein indicated that this would not be a problem.

As they all exited the office, Stein's pulled Jake to the back of the car wash.

"I spoke to Bob Branson. He does not want me doing business with the broad. I just do business with you. She can come, but you must be there"

"You got it man" Jake quietly mouthed to Stein, patting him on the shoulder and then walked out to his car.

As Tania and Jake pulled out of the lot, Jake pointed to his wire and indicated to Tania to turn hers off. Jake did the same.

"Shit, we got him" Jake said. "You know, I kinda feel sorry for the guy. I've been working with him for over a year now and he's not a bad guy, stupid but not bad. He's got no idea what's coming."

Tania looked incredulously at him,

"You got to be kidding me Jake. The lives he's ruining with that stuff. I can't believe you feel that way. The sooner we get him off the streets the better. My office will want me to do one more buy at a higher quantity before we can arrest him".

"That may be difficult. He just told me that he will only work with me from now on"

"We'll figure this out Jake. Just don't be going soft on me" Tania smiled as she patted his hand.

Jake dropped her off at the Garden City office and headed into Manhattan. He needed to get the white powder in the brown paper bag into evidence as quickly as possible. 26 Federal Plaza was deserted once he arrived with just a few covering officers manning each of the bureaus. Once all the evidence was taken and documentation finished, Jake left the building. It was already dark and the snow was coming down at a steady rate.

Chapter Three

It was brutal trying to get home from the busy streets of Manhattan. This was the final official work day before Christmas for many New York employees. As he sat in traffic, Jake decided to meet some of his buddies from the Federal Building in Manhattan who he knew would be celebrating down at the local, Poets Corner Public House. He pulled off the main road and after winding in and out of numerous side streets, he parked his government car three streets over from the public house. If he was caught using his government car for anything other than government business, it would be an immediate 45-day suspension.

He jogged through the wet snow until he burst through the saloon doors. Everyone turned around to see Jake bedraggled and panting in the doorway.

"What the fuck" a voice came from the back of the room. "Were your ears burning, we were just talking about you. Get over here Jake. Merry Christmas"

Rick and half a dozen of his colleagues welcomed Jake demanding to know what was happening. Hours later, Jake stumbled out of the doors and tried to remember which direction he had parked his car. The traffic had gone, the streets quiet. Jakes head hit the pillow in his condo. How he had got home, he couldn't remember. He did remember that he had promised to pick his mother to go shopping the following morning at nine am. He had four hours to sober up.

Christmas dinner was at Jake's sister's house. He arrived to find his sister Eunice already arguing with her daughter Jess about the seating arrangements. The family arrived one by one. Joe, Eunice's husband, had already hit the bottle in desperation and was sat outside on a plastic chair on the porch. The snow was coming down hard. Jake pulled up a chair next to him and left the rest of the family yelling at each other. Kate, another sister, banged on the front door indicating that dinner was ready. Jake and Joe looked at each other, shook hands and walked inside. The table was laid with a Christmas Ham in the center and various Christmas dishes from each of the family lay close to the ham. It was a feast to behold. Jakes mother sat at the head of the table and was trying to get everyone's attention. Eventually all four feet nine inches of her stood up as she yelled,

"Jesus Mary and Joseph, sit down"

Everyone found their seats. Just before Grace was about to be said, one of the sisters remarked loudly that she was not happy with the seating arrangements. The discussion got louder and louder until one sister announced they were leaving. Bedlam ensued, Joe and Jake quietly left the table, resumed their positions on the plastic chairs, clinked their plastic mugs full of wine and watched the snow fall at their feet. Another Christmas to remember!

December 30th 1986 marked Jake's 41st birthday. It was 7:30pm and Jake was about to leave his condo to meet friends for dinner when the phone rang. Stein identified himself and said that he was calling from the home of Bob Branson. He told Jake that he had just picked up an extra ounce of cocaine and that Tania could have it for $2000 that evening. Jake told him that he would call Tania to see if she wanted it. Before they hung up, Stein told Jake that he would have to be present.

Jake called Tania at home. Tania's sister answered the phone and told Jake that Tania was out of town for the New Years' celebration. Knowing that he could not get the cash together that quickly, Jake called Stein and told him about Tania. Sounding annoyed, Stein indicated he was also taking a trip and would not be available till February. Jake informed him that Tania wanted a quarter pound of Cocaine. It was agreed that when they met in February, they could do the complete deal. They arranged to speak at the beginning of February which seemed to satisfy Stein. Jake wrote a brief note and then headed out the door to celebrate his birthday.

Jake took the Long Island Bullet Train to Manhattan where he was meeting a few of his Agent buddies to celebrate his birthday. A new mandate had come out due to the shortage of gas. The mandate required all Agents to leave their government cars in the Federal Building garage every week night and for the entire weekend. Jake met Rick, his buddy and his partner at Poets Corner. They had one drink and walked to to a Manhattan night club where they had arranged to meet another Agent, Keith Lenney.

It was late when they left the club. It was pouring with rain and the wind was whipping through the tall buildings of Manhattan.

"Screw this, I'm going to get my government car. I'm not getting the train in this weather"

Rick agreed but Keith said his goodbyes as he was bunking with a friend in Manhattan, for the night.

Rick and Jake found Jake's car and drive slowly out of the parking garage. The rain was turning to sleet as they slowly made their way out of Manhattan, bound for Long Island. They were creeping along at 15 miles per hour, when the car in front slammed on his brakes and Jake's car "caressed" the back of the car in front. Jake backed up, put the bubble light on top of the car and overtook the driver. As they passed the driver and passenger, Rick gestured to them to pull over under an upcoming bridge. Somewhat sheltered by the bridge from the sleet, Jake got out of the car and walked towards the other vehicle. The driver got out with his hands in the air.

"It's ok Officer, I understand. The roads are so slippery."

Jake and the driver walked to the back of the car where there was no damage. Jake's car was also undamaged.

"Hey no harm, no foul" Jake declared. "Just give me your name and address in case I should need it. I'm not going to call this in as there is no damage"

From the passenger seat he heard a female voice,

"Jeff, I have to get home".

Jeff Kinsler quickly gave Jake his details and then hurried back to his car.

The following day was New Years Eve, a short day at the office. He walked into the office and was immediately called into Ted Caturo's office.

"Did something happen last night" Ted asked.

"No sir"

"I believe you were in your government car conducting a surveillance, right? Conducting a surveillance, correct? Ted went on purposely nodding his head up and down.

"Yes sir, that's correct" Jake replied slowly.

"An attorney has called in this morning stating that you hit her client's car. Initially you drove off and then came back to the scene and intimidated the driver into not reporting the accident. You are being accused of a hit and run" Ted relayed.

"That's absolutely not the case" Jake replied shaking his head.

He recounted the story to Ted Caturo, stating that Rick was a witness to what happened.

"I'm sorry Jake. This has to be investigated by the Office of Personnel Responsibility. Until then you are grounded and cannot drive a government vehicle."

Jake shook his head, undoubtedly Valerio would be involved in this investigation.

"Jake you might as well finish up any paperwork and head home" Ted added.

Jake left his supervisors office, signed a few papers and headed back to Long Island on the Long Island Bullet Train. He was back at his condo by 11:30am. He picked up his personal car and headed out to pay a visit to Mr. Jeff Kinsler at his home address.

He knocked on the door at the address he had been given the previous night. Jeff answered the door and immediately went as white as a ghost.

Jeff walked out of the door and closed it behind him.

"I'm sorry man. My best friend is an attorney. It was his idea. He ran your plates last night and they came back unknown. He figured it was a government car and that there may be money if he pursued it" Jake blurted out.

"Well let me tell you what happened to me." Jake recounted his visit with his supervisor earlier that morning.

"That woman in the car with you, she wasn't your wife was she?" Jake asked lowering his voice.

"No man, oh God"

"The truth will come out and she will be questioned. You need to recant your statements and your attorney needs to withdraw the complaint." Jake advised.

"Will I be in trouble for embellishing the story?" Jeff asked.

"No, you just need to come forward with the truth and quickly."

"I'm sorry man" Jeff called to Jake as he walked towards his car.

"Yeah yeah. Happy New Year." Jake got in his car and headed back to the condo.

The snow was coming down as he negotiated the icy streets. He passed a car pulled over to the side with a flat tire. The trunk was open and a black woman was peering inside. Jake pulled over and asked the lady if she needed help. She explained that she had a flat but no spare tire. Jake identified himself and showed the lady his credentials. He asked if he could give her a lift home. She immediately accepted. As they got closer to her home the lady asked if Jake could drop her a block before the house. She explained that her husband would give her a beating if he saw her in a car with a white man. Jake felt sickened as the lady got out of his warm car into the snow and the cold howling wind. The lady turned, smiled and gave a Jake a wave before slowly walking in the direction of her home.

Two days later, Jake heard that Jeff Kinsler had followed through with his recant of the accident and his attorney withdrew the complaint.

The entire month of January, 1987 Jake spent sat at his desk getting the documentation, wire tapes and photographs ready for the imminent arrest of Stein. By early February Stein still hadn't been in touch. Slightly panicked, Jake requested permission to drop by the car wash to see if he could find out what was going on.

There was a huge line of cars covered in slush and salt from the roads waiting to get into the car wash. Jake pulled past them all and parked in the rear of the lot.

"Where's your boss" Jake shouted over to one of the kids drying a vehicle with towels

.

"Try the office" he yelled back.

Jake walked into the lobby and found Stein's partner Jeff Casein taking apart the cash register. He lifted his head, looked at Jake,

"Piece of junk! It always acts up when we're busy. Are you looking for Mike?"

"Yeah" Jake replied "Haven't seen him forever! Where's he hiding"?

"He's in the Hamptons. One of his buddy's kids is getting married so he decided to stay on for a while longer. Should be back in town next week!'.

"Have him give me a call when he gets back. It's Jake Taylor".

"I know who you are Special Agent"

Jake returned to the office to update his files. Within the hour, Stein called him,

"Are you missing me Jake"

"Call me on this number in five minutes" Jake retorted and gave him the seven digits.

"Where've you been Mike. I've got Tania on my back expecting 4 ounces of Coke"

"Relax man, I got it. I'm still in the Hamptons. I'll be back in town on Monday. I'll need the money up front. $7500. I don't have the cash to front this right now."

"Jesus Mike. There's no way she's going to give you $7500 before she sees the product. You're not dealing with an amateur here"

"You need to make it happen Jake. You know I'm good for it".

"I know, but she doesn't. She doesn't trust you, just as you don't trust her. I'll talk to her. Call me Monday when you get back into town"

Jake hung up and immediately called Tania.

"We've got a way in."

Jake explained to Tania what had transpired in his phone call with Stein.

"I figure that we could make a deal where I go in with $4000 in the morning of the deal and then you insist that you be present later the same day, to see the product and pay the $3500 balance". Jake crossed his fingers hoping that Tania would agree.

"Let me run it past my boss first. We could put a tail on Stein after you give him the $4000. I don't trust that slimy bastard".

"I do" Jake immediately replied. "This is what we need to do. Shit we are almost there".

"I'll get back to you Jake" Tania hung up.

As plans were made for the final drug meet, Jake needed to ensure everything was ready for the case to move forward. He mailed the final alien registration cards to Lorenzo Endario and Jusieppi D'Abrevio. He called Stein and arranged to meet him at the car wash to provide him with the passports of the Israeli citizens with temporary Alien Registration numbers and expiration dates. Jake made the excuse that he would have to drop the passports off and leave quickly as he needed to be in a meeting.

He entered the lobby of the car wash at 3pm on April 13th, 1987. Diana was behind the counter and immediately grabbed Jake's hand and walked him to the back office. She whispered in his ear,

"Thanks for being such a good friend to my husband. He thinks the world of you"

Jake smiled at her and then walked into the office. He gave the passports to Stein smiled and said,

"Gotta go, see you at the next".

He quickly excited the car wash and met his back up Fred Lamar at the Garden City Office to review and confer what had just taken place.

That night, at home, Jake received a phone call at home from Stein.

"What's going on Jake" he demanded.

"I've no idea what you are talking about" Jake quipped back. Had someone blown the operation? Did Stein know what was coming?

"You're getting lazy man. It's almost Memorial Day. The beautiful people will be heading to the Hamptons. They need their fixes. Are you getting soft on me? Do I need to find a new distributor"?

"Jesus Mike. I already have you getting 4 ounces for Tania"

"That's for the broad. What about you?

"I got to be careful Mike. I can't raise too much suspicion. Anyway Tania wouldn't be happy if she knew I was going into competition with her for the Hamptons"

"Shit Jake. Don't give me that bullshit! The Hamptons are packed on Memorial Day weekend. Way enough demand for the two of you".

"I'll think about it. I'm short of cash right now" he replied, trying to placate Stein.

"If you were doing your job, you wouldn't be short of cash. Getting lazy man"

The phone clicked off.

For the rest of April, Jake was detailed to JFK airport to assist with ongoing investigations. As he was already familiar working the airport, he knew most of the Agents and this was a welcome break from Adonis. The office had received intelligence that a female transporting cocaine, was on an inbound flight from Columbia. In plain clothes, the agents mingled with the passengers coming off the jet and made their way with the crowd down to baggage claim. A DEA sniffer dog had screened all the baggage with no hit, so both Custom Agents and the DEA agents were on high alert for "swallowers" and anything else unusual. Jake spoke to the cabin attendants to see if any passengers had refused drinks or food during the flight. If there was a passenger on board who has swallowed packages of drugs, they would not ingest anything so to slow the digestion process down. This would allow them to make it off the plane and out of the airport before the drugs would make it to their large intestine. He also questioned if any of the passengers had become ill during the flight, this was a possibility should one of the swallowed bags burst within the body causing a massive overdose. The attendants offered no information to substantiate a swallower on board.

Jake radioed the information to baggage claim and proceeded to the lower level to join his fellow agents. He entered the elevator and held the door open for a larger lady wearing a thick fur coat who was moving very slowly. Jake watched the lady as she searched her purse for a handkerchief to mop her brow and red face. They arrived at baggage level and Jake once again held the door open for her as she exited the elevator.

The lady walked towards the carousel with the bags from the Colombian flight. Jake followed at a distance as she slowly approached the moving belt and positioned herself against a wall which she then leaned on heavily. By this time, many of the bags had been claimed. Suddenly she leaned forward and picked up a small black case and then leaned back on the wall.

Jake approached the lady and asked if there was anything he could do to help her. She shook her head and mopped her brow again.

Jake identified himself and asked her if she would like to sit down and remove her coat while he called for some help for her.

"No no gracias. I am very well thank you" she panted in very broken English.

"Por favor, sientate. Please sit down" Jake insisted and almost carried her to a nearby chair. He alerted a colleague and asked for a wheelchair. He also asked for a medical team to be called.

"No, no, gracias. I am very well" the lady kept repeating.

Although refusing help, it was quite obvious to all present, that she would be unable to get back up from the chair without help. As the medical team assisted her into the wheelchair and removed the heavy coat, Jake spoke to his colleagues and shared his suspicion of the lady concealing drugs on her body hidden by the fur coat. The sniffer dog was brought to the scene, immediately barked and sat down next to the lady, indicating a positive hit. The team transported the lady into the customs offices behind baggage claim and informed her of their suspicions, via an interpreter.

During a search, bags of cocaine were found sewn into her thighs. The lady who was now complaining of terrible pain, almost seemed relieved to be caught. When questioned after the surgery to remove the drugs, she revealed she had been paid five hundred US dollars to carry the drugs. She also explained how her family was now at risk from the drug dealers as she had failed the mission.

Jake wrote up the arrest and prepared it for the DEA office at the other side of the airport. As the lady was been transported to a local hospital, it was critical that the arrest be filed quickly. The supervisor told Jake to take a customs car and drive the perimeter of the airport to the DEA office. Jake had done this numerous times and had taken the safe driving airport course on two separate occasions. Still high from the arrest, Jake came to a four way stop on the tarmac. To the right of him was a large 747 jet. From his position, Jake could see the captain in his cockpit through the plane's window. The captain saluted

Jake, which Jake misinterpreted as a sign for him to proceed first. Both the plane and Jake's car moved simultaneously followed by both vehicles coming to a sudden stop. The captain of the plane raised his arms as the passengers were thrown forward and back again in their seats. Jake gave a quick wave, bowed his head and drove on his way. Within seconds, there was a call over the radio for the driver of Jake's custom's car to report to the Airport Manager's office immediately. The following day Jake attended a third airport safe driving course and, under protest, wrote a long letter of apology to the captain of the plane he had "cut off."

May 11th 1987 was the second unseasonably warm day. It has snowed the previous week, now everyone around the office wore short sleeved shirts and the general mood was upbeat. Jake, on the other hand, was jumpy and nervous. Today was the day that he would meet Stein at the car wash with a $4000 deposit on a quarter pound of cocaine. It had been agreed that Jake would meet with Stein on his own today and then Tania and Jake would meet him the following day with the final payment of $3500. This was the beginning of the end. Jake had been introduced to Adonis in January 1986. He had lived and breathed Adonis for the past 15 months. He couldn't believe it was almost over.

He checked his wiretap three times and went over the route twice, with his back up team, Lemar and Sands. Ted Caturo, his supervisor would also be listening to his conversation with Stein as it happened.

Caturo slapped Jake on the back as he walked out of the office,

"Give it hell" his parting words

"Hey, no pressure" Jake yelled over his shoulder without looking back.

Another long line of cars waited outside the car wash. The first couple of nice days and everyone wanted their cars washed, thought Jake as he pulled into the back of the lot.

This time he carried his briefcase into the lobby. He walked straight back into the small office at the back of the lobby. Stein was sat at his desk on the phone. He waved to Jake as he sat in the only other chair next to the file cabinet. Jake tried to look calm as his stomach did somersaults inside. He was ready to take

Stein down but at the same time felt sorry for what he was about to do.

"Jake, Jake, Jake my man" Stein leaned back in his chair and put his feet on the desk,

"You got my money"

Jake opened the briefcase and removed eight wads of $500 in twenty dollar notes.

"$4000 of hard earned money my friend. Let's hope this $4000 will bring us far more in returns"

"No shit" grinned Stein. "I'm heading over to Bob's tonight with Diana for dinner. She's hoping for the weather to stay warm so we can take a walk on the beach. Jesus, pray for rain"

Jake stood up, shook Stein's hand grinning

"It's going to be a gorgeous evening. Take your flip flops"

"Get outta here" Stein quipped as Jake walked out through the lobby. "See you at three tomorrow".

"Let's do this Jake" Tania smiled and got out of the passenger door of Jake's government car. May 12th, 1987 was the polar opposite of the day before. The rain was pouring down. It was a dark crappy day, which mirrored Jakes mood.

The car wash was empty, a new cash register sat unused on the counter in the lobby.

Jake ushered Tania into Stein's office.

Stein nodded at Tania and shook Jake's hand. Getting right to business, Stein pointed to the file cabinet looking at Jake,

"Your product is in the top drawer".

Jake reached over, opening the drawer and handed a brown paper bag to Tania. Tania took the bag and placed it in her open palm as if trying to weigh it.

"It's all there" Stein quickly commented. "It's real high-quality product, just like the other".

"I'm sure it is Mr. Stein. My clients have been very pleased up to now. I hope we can make this a regular thing" Tania smiled at Stein.

Obviously uncomfortable, Stein looked at Jake with a sarcastic look on his face,

"We only supply the best of the best, don't we Jake. Just don't understand why others don't take advantage of the goods"

"That's right. True professionals" Jake felt sick.

Tania inspected the white powder before returning it to Jake. She opened her large purse and removed an envelope. She handed the envelope to Stein adding,

"I think you will find it all there. It's been a pleasure doing business", she paused, looked at Jake and continued "doing business with you both"

Back at the office, everyone clapped as Tania and Jake walked through the door. The Resident Agent in Charge beckoned for Tania and Jake to come into his office. He opened one of his cabinets and produced an expensive looking bottle of Scotch and three glasses. He poured a healthy glass for each of them and proposed a toast.

"Here's to success and a hell of a lot of work".

The days leading up to May 27th, 1987 dragged on and on for Jake. He helped other Agents with ongoing investigations to pass the time. A younger Agent approached him in the office that morning and asked if Jake would help him serve a complaint to a local man who had been using his large dog to intimidate people. There was also a complaint from neighbors in the building stating that the dog barked all day and night. It soon became apparent that the young Agent was petrified of dogs.

"No problem" Jake answered grabbing his coat.

He peaked around Ted Caturo's door.

"Boss, I'm just going to help Agent Kerber talk to a local about a complaint". Ted nodded in agreement as he answered his phone.

"Let's go" he said to Agent Kerber. "We'll take my car"

They arrived at a Tudor building on the outskirts of Garden City, formerly the Garden City Hotel which had been renovated into plush private condominiums.

"It's the fourth floor" Agent Kerber advised.

Jake flashed his credentials at the doorman and headed to the stairs. They found the condo and knocked on the door. There was no reply and all was quiet. As they walked down the stairs, they heard loud barking.

Mr. Frank Delaney was walking through the lobby holding the leash of a large Rottweiler.

Jake looked at Agent Kerber. All the color had drained from his face. Obviously, he was not going to talk anytime soon.

"Mr. Frank Delaney, I presume" Jake flashed his credentials. "My name is Special Agent Taylor. We need to talk. Shall we do this in private?"

Frank walked past Jake and indicated for Jake and Agent Kerber to follow. Once again, they walked the four flights up to the apartment. Frank opened the door and the three of them entered. Jake was sure to leave the door open should they have to make a hasty retreat.

"Mr. Delaney, we have a number of complaints about you using your dog to intimidate your neighbors, plus we have a noise complaint from your dog barking."

"Really and what do you intend to do about these complaints Officers?" As Frank spoke, he pulled on the leash causing the dog to growl.

Jake opened his jacket to reveal his weapon.

"Mr. Delaney, I suggest you secure your dog or I will shoot it if it comes one step closer to me"

Frank turned and secured the dog's leash to the radiator.

"We would like you to report to the Garden City INS office this afternoon at 2pm for questioning. Here is the paperwork with the address. If you cannot make it this afternoon, or you wish to have an attorney present, please call this number and reschedule".

"My wife is an attorney" Frank replied

"That's good. We will see you this afternoon. Thank you for your cooperation."

With that Jake and Agent Kerber backed out of the apartment, without taking their eyes off the dog. As the front door shut, they both sighed with relief.

Agent Kerber took off running down the stairs whereas Jake took a more leisurely pace.

Back in the vehicle, a message blurted out over the radio,

"Anyone in the vicinity of the former Garden City Hotel, please radio in and return to the Garden City INS office immediately".

Jake radioed in and headed back to the office.

The two Agents reported immediately to Supervisor Ted Caturo's office.

"Jesus, what happened with you two" Ted stood up from behind his desk.

"Nothing exciting Boss. We served a complaint at the home of Frank Delaney and advised him to report to this office for questioning. Under the circumstances, it went quite smoothly, didn't it Agent Kerber" Jake turned to Agent Kerber.

"Better than expected" reported Agent Kerber.

"Well, I just heard differently from a very irate wife, Attorney Delaney. She claims that you drew your gun, had him down on the ground and threatened both him and his dog" Ted relayed.

Before Jake had time to reply, Agent Kerber spoke up,

"That's absolutely not true Sir. If anything, Frank Delaney tried to menace us with his nasty Rottweiler. Neither of us pulled a gun and at no point was Mr, Delaney asked to lay on the ground".

"Your word against hers" Ted replied. "Another damn OPR investigation and the two of you are grounded".

The following day was a Saturday. Jake took his personal vehicle and drove over to the former Garden

City Hotel. This time he wore jeans, a sweater, a ball cap and sunglasses.

He entered the building, flashed his credentials at the same doorman and proceeded to the second floor. There were two condo doors that he knocked on, but no reply. He then headed to the third floor, again two condo doors. The first was opened by a young woman who advised that she had been at work yesterday as Jake asked if she had heard anything around 11:00 am.

Jake then knocked on the other condo door which was promptly opened by an old lady with white hair.

"Excuse Ma'am. My name is Agent Jake Taylor"

The lady cut him off mid-sentence and said

"I know who you are. You had better come in"

She gestured to Jake to sit down at the kitchen table while she put the kettle on. Jake looked around and saw a framed picture of an older man in a NYPD uniform.

"I'm Nettie Bond, that's my husband Bob. He passed away two years ago. He was a Captain with the NYPD. Worked there all his life, retired from the job after almost 40 years."

She poured two cups of tea and set one down in front of Jake and one on the table in front of where she sat down.

"Sugar" she asked.

Jake replied "No Ma'am thank you".

"Please call me Nettie"

"Ok Nettie, only if you will call me Jake"

She nodded in agreement.

"I'm here to see if you heard anything yesterday around 11am".

"Jake. Once a cop's wife, always a cop's wife. I heard the whole thing, from you knocking on Frank Delaney's door with no reply, to when you left after talking to him and his rotten dog".

Jake told Nettie what had transpired in Ted Caturo's office.

"That never happened" Nettie stated indignantly. "Those people are all trouble. They cause so many problems here. People believe her because she is an attorney. They listen to him because he has that awful beast of a dog"

"Mrs. oops, I mean Nettie, would you be willing to swear an affidavit stating everything you witnessed and heard yesterday".

"Absolutely" Nettie replied "We can't let these people get away with this. I will bring my affidavit down to the Garden City INS office on Monday myself and ask to speak with Mr. Caturo."

"That's not necessary" Jake replied.

"Oh yes, it is. I will have Fred the doorman drive me down there. I don't get out that much these days".

"Ok, that's settled then" Jake stood up and held his hand out for Nettie to shake.

She also stood up and clasped his hand with both her hands.

"You remind me of my Bob. He would do whatever it took to get the truth. It's been a pleasure meeting you. Perhaps if you are ever in the area again, you could stop in for a cup of tea".

"You betcha I will Nettie. It was great to meet you also"

On Monday, true to her word, Nettie Bond showed up at the Garden City INS office, affidavit in hand. Jake and Agent Kerber were back in business again.

Although busy getting all the evidence for the US Attorney, Jake dreaded what was about to happen yet he also knew it was time. The warrant for Stein's arrest was issued on May 25th, 1987 in the Eastern District of New York based on the complaint filed charging Michael Stein with Violation of Title 21 U.S.C 841 (A) (1) Distribution of Cocaine.

It was decided that Jake would contact Stein that same Monday and set up a meeting on May 27th at

10am at Lister Park. The reason given would be to talk about further purchases of Cocaine. Jake would not be wearing a wire, however, the signal for the arresting team comprising of twelve FBI agents would be Jake opening the trunk of his vehicle from the switch on his front dashboard of his government car. Jake would also be arrested to maintain his cover.

Jake pulled into the parking lot of Lister Park, Valley Stream at approximately 9:50am. It had been preplanned for Jake to park in an end parking space making it difficult should Stein wanted to run. Within five minutes Stein arrived. Jake opened his driver's side window and beckoned Stein to join him in his vehicle.

Stein sat in the passenger seat and immediately started in on Jake.

"This is ridiculous man. You've missed the Memorial Day weekend crowd. I'm seriously thinking we should go our separate ways"

Without answering, Jake hit the trunk switch. Stein turned and gave Jake a look which would remain with him for years to come. It was a look of fear, betrayal and anger. Before he could speak, the car was surrounded by FBI agents. Both Jake and Stein were pulled out of the car and thrown face down to the tarmac. With guns drawn, Stein was told to put his hands behind his back. He was cuffed and pulled up to a standing position. He had obviously urinated in fear as the front of his pants was wet. He was walked to an awaiting vehicle and assisted into the back seat. The car drove away and Jake was assisted to his feet.

Stein was taken to the Garden City office for processing and fingerprinting. He was advised of his rights and given a copy of a FD-395 Advice of Rights form to read. Stein advised that he understood his rights but refused to sign the form loudly proclaiming his innocence. He was then transported to Eastern District, Brooklyn, New York where he was arraigned before a United States Magistrate. He was released on $100,000 bond and ordered to return to court on June 24th, 1987 for a preliminary hearing.

Jake was half expecting a phone call at his home from Stein, but it never came. At this point Stein still believed that Jake was a dirty agent. This would soon change when Stein's attorney, Benjamin Pello with his client visited the US Attorney for the Eastern District of New York, Anthony Morgan. The photographic evidence, wire tapes and telephone conversations recorded by Jake were played to Stein and Pello. It became quite clear that the US Attorney had a water tight case.

The previously vocal Stein was silenced and Attorney Pello sat back and listened as Attorney Morgan explained that they intended to request a sentence of 30 years for the crimes committed. Stein remained silent and stone faced as Pello stated that his client would be interested in a deal to reduce his prison sentence. Attorney Morgan said he would put together a deal whereby Stein would fully cooperate with the FBI, DEA and INS. Once Stein's cooperation was proven he would be able to plead to a lesser crime. The preliminary hearing scheduled for June 24th was put on hold and the parties agreed that they would meet again in one month after Stein had met with the federal agencies.

Jake was now under the impression that his work with Stein was coming to an end. He would have to attend and testify in the court trial as a witness as well as follow up with warrants for the individuals who had attained Alien Registration cards as a result of the undercover work. As this detail concluded, he knew he would have to return to his office within the FBI in Manhattan, however it was agreed that he would continue working with the INS in Garden City until the arrests associated with the violation of the Federal Bribery Statute and the Alien Registration cards were complete and the case concluded in Court. It was also agreed that the INS could detail him out to their agencies should the need arise.

His first detail was with Secret Service. It was to arrest a prominent Wall Street business man for child pornography. Mr. Flynn had recently travelled to Mexico City to visit his brother. During his visit, he had taken pornographic naked pictures of his young niece, unbeknownst to his brother. Upon his arrival back to New York, Mr. Flynn had taken the film to be processed at a local One Hour Photo store. The manager of the One Hour Photo developed the film and immediately reported its contents to Secret Service. Jake's partner, Jayne Smith, was also assigned to Secret Service. They met at the Manhattan INS office the day the warrant was issued. They agreed to meet at 4:30am the following day at the office.

Manhattan was deserted as they drove together to the address on the warrant. It turned out to be a Penthouse apartment on Park Avenue. The doorman was snoozing in a chair as they entered the building. He stood up, brushed himself down with his hand,

"Good morning" he croaked as Jake showed him his FBI credentials.

" Good morning. We need access to the Penthouse and they better be surprised to see us" Jake looked straight at the doorman and raised his eyebrows.

The doorman coughed and cleared his throat.

"You will have no trouble from me, Officers. Come this way to the elevators. I will put in the code which will take you right up to the 15th floor"

Jake nodded at the doorman and followed him to the elevator.

It was 5 am sharp as Jayne banged on the door to the penthouse suite.

"Easy" Jake whispered to Jayne "We want him alive, not dead from a heart attack".

"Can I help you?" a loud males voice was heard from behind the door. Jake put his credentials up against the peep hole in the door. FBI can we please come in"

A key in the lock could be heard turning and the door opened to reveal a tall and thin white male approximately 50 years old, in a burgundy robe.

"Mr. Flynn, Mark Robert Flynn?" Jake questioned

"Yes, yes that's me"

A female voice could be heard behind him,

"Who is it Mark?"

"It's the FBI" he replied

Mrs Margaret Flynn came to the door,

"What is it, what happened" she said with obvious anxiety in her voice.

Jake began to speak,

"Mr. Mark Robert Flynn, I have a warrant for your arrest...."

From behind him Jayne yelled,

"On the ground now. On the ground" Jake turned to see her holding her gun pointed at Mr Flynn.

Before Jake could say anything, Jayne grabbed Mr. Flynn and threw him on the ground.

"Jesus, Jayne. Where is he going to run to, we are on the 15th floor. Put the damn gun away. Mr. Flynn you are to accompany us to the Manhattan FBI office where you will be processed for your arrest. Are there any guns in the apartment?"

"Yes, in my office desk" Mark Flynn whispered. "Why am I being arrested?"

"Ok Mrs. Flynn. Why don't you take a seat and let's make this easy for everyone. Mr. Flynn, let's go to your office"

Jayne followed as Jake found the loaded gun in the office desk. He rendered it harmless, put the bullets in his pocket and replaced the gun in the desk.

"Now Mr. Flynn. Thank you for your cooperation. You are being arrested for child pornography. I will now read you your rights. We are going to be together for the next twelve hours. Please go wash your face and brush your teeth. Put on some loose comfortable clothing and your shoes and we will leave together" Jake made it sound like an invitation.

Mark Flynn listened as Jake rattled off his Miranda warning from memory. He then walked sheepishly into the bathroom and left the door ajar.

"Are you not going in there with him?" Jayne demanded to know.

"Jayne, where is he going to go? Think about it, we are on the 15th floor. Believe me, we want this guy to brush his teeth before we leave. I hate morning breath".

Mark Flynn cooperated and emerged from his bedroom wearing work out sweats and sneakers.

"Do you have a jacket" Jake asked.

Mrs. Flynn stood up from the sofa,

"I'll get it. She opened a door off the hallway and retrieved a jacket"

Jake told Mark Flynn he would have to handcuff him and to hold out his hands.

Mark complied while Jake loosely placed the handcuffs and then took the jacket from Mrs. Flynn and looped it over Mark's hands, concealing the cuffs.

"Let's go" Jake stood behind Jake as they walked to the door.

"Here is my card, Mrs Flynn. Give me about an two hours and then call me. I will tell you what is happening and when you will be able to see your husband."

"Am I allowed to kiss him goodbye?"

Jayne rolled her eyes, already knowing the answer.

"Absolutely" Jake replied.

Once Jake and Jayne had fingerprinted and processed Mr. Flynn, Jake placed him in a single holding cell awaiting interview. Jake turned to Jayne,

"Let's go outside to talk"

"What the hell Jayne. Do you think you may have come on a little too heavy?" Jake demanded,

"Absolutely not" Jayne replied indigently. "He's a criminal and should be treated as such"

"What happened to innocent until proven guilty?" Jake replied.

Jayne's face flushed,

"I believe in protecting myself as well as my prisoner"

"Ok Agent Smith. This will be the last time we work together. Remember this is probably the worst day in this mans' life. He's about to loose everything, including his freedom. Justice will be served, but not by us. He cooperated with us. We need to always act in a professional manner".

Jake turned around and walked back into Federal Plaza.

He later found out that before Secret Service, Jayne had worked as a prison guard at Rykers Island. He never did work with her again.

His next detail also involved Secret Service. President Ronald Reagan was coming to New York to meet with Mayor Ed Koch.

Jake was detailed to Secret Service to assist in security during the President's visit. Jake had great respect for Reagan and so eagerly awaited his orders.

When the orders came in, his excitement was soon deflated as his assignment was to watch a manhole cover in Times Square. This, with his partner, Agent Terri Stevens, he did for 12 long hours and never did see the President.

He decided if this was the last association with Secret Service, it would be fine with him.

Chapter Four

Ted Caturo, Jake's INS detail supervisor, called Jake into his office. He explained that he owed a favor to the DEA office in Brooklyn. The Brooklyn Agent in Charge had heard about Jake's recent successes and requested Jake to work on a detail they had been working for over eight months. At the same time Jake would assist in the training of a new young federal agent assigned to the same detail.

Jake received the synopsis of the detail, code name Arctic Frost, that same afternoon. Eight months prior, credible intel had been received by the DEA office, regarding a container which was being stored at a dock yard in Brooklyn. The informant had stated that the container contained five tons of cocaine which was to be distributed in the Miami area.

Since inception, Arctic Frost had employed 12 DEA agents surveilling the container, twenty-four hours a day, seven days a week. Observation points were from both vehicles and dock yard buildings. A tracking device had also been placed on the container.

Recent new intel suggested that the container was to be moved in the next four weeks to its destination in Florida. Jake was to join Arctic Frost as the back up for the Case Officer in Charge. His partner, Scott Engel, was a brand-new rookie with the FBI who had also been detailed to the DEA.

Jake met Agent Scott Engel at the DEA office in Brooklyn. Scott's enthusiasm for the case brought back memories for Jake from when he started at the Justice Department. As they headed to the garage to pick up the undercover vehicle, Scott rambled on about how excited he was to join the Arctic Frost Taskforce and that he hoped he was up for the job. His hope was that he was on shift the day the container moved and that he would be able to follow it to its destination in Miami. Jake took the driver's seat, turned to Scott and told him to prepare for the most boring time in his life.

"Let's see how you feel after watching this container for a month. You will not leave the vehicle for eight hours. You will pee in a cup and pray that nature is on your side and that's all you have to do in a cup. You will eat, drink and live in this car for eight hours. You will take countless photographs and even videos of this container doing absolutely nothing. Most of all, and let me emphasize that again. Most of all, you will pray that you are not in this car when the tracking device on the container alarms, because if that happens, you will learn how to clean your teeth in a cup, shave in the rear-view mirror, all the time with one eyeball on the container."

After the first two weeks, Scott and Jake knew everything about each other. Although from entirely different backgrounds, they found a mutual respect for each other and developed a friendship which would last for the entirety of Jake's career.

The mind-blowing tedium and monotony eventually squashed Scott's enthusiasm. Monday morning of week three all hell broke loose. It was 7:30am. A large semi-truck cab reversed and hooked up to the front of the container, while the tracking device alarmed over the radio. The Case Agent in charge of the surveillance was off site, so Jake who was second in command, declared over the radio, for all agents on site to keep an eyeball on the container and to follow the container wherever it went. He radioed into the office and requested air support and finally spoke to the Case Agent to discuss the plan. Case Agent Annie Udell advised Jake that she would contact the FBI team involved with this case. She also advised Jake to always remain in radio contact.

The truck cab, hooked up to the container, rolled slowly out of the dusty dock yard causing a fog of dust and dirt. Jake struggled to see out of the window as Scott, in the driver's seat, tried to grapple with the windshield wipers to try and get the wiper wash to operate. This caused a thick layer of mud to form on the window.

"Keep going" Jake shouted as he grabbed a sweater out of the back seat, opened his passenger window and leaned out to try and clean the windshield.

"Jesus Jake, get back in the car. I need you to get me through this, not dead at the side of the road. Wait till we get a red light, will ya"

Jake manipulated his body back into the passenger seat. Mud all over his forearms. He'd managed to clean a little window in the mud, enough for Scott to see the road ahead.

"This is C42. Whose got an eyeball" he yelled into the radio.

"C15, we have him in our sights"

"C23, we see him also"

Jake radioed into the office,

"He's heading to Interstate 278, my guess to the Verrazano Bridge. Notify New Jersey that he is heading there way"

"Clear C42." Annie Udell replied "I'm in a chopper heading your way. I will coordinate with New Jersey. I will join the detail with the New Jersey team and take over command"

"Thank God" Jake whispered.

He turned to Scott,

"We are heading to Miami my friend"

Traffic was at a crawl over the Verrazano Bridge. Scott slipped in behind a vehicle while Jake got out of the car and ran alongside cleaning the window. The truck and container sailed right on through the truck payment kiosks while many of the agents sat in line at the car payment kiosks. Jake waited a couple of minutes and then instructed Scott to drive through the truck kiosk lane. He did so to the chorus of loud truck horns blasting behind them. Jake showed his credentials to the kiosk worker and they were back tucked in behind the container.

At the "Welcome to New Jersey" sign, the New York agents were contacted by Case Agent Annie Udell and told to continue the surveillance but to fall back. This was to allow the New Jersey undercover agents to move in behind the container. She radioed Jake and told him that she would meet him at the container's first stop, which happened to be East Brunswick, New Jersey. The truck and container pulled in to to diesel pumps. Jake confirmed over the radio that more than one car had eyeballs on the truck and container, then pulled over to an area behind the Mini-store and rendezvoused with Annie Udell. Scott took the opportunity to use the bathroom and buy two small coffees, two donuts, two packs of gum and a pack of breath mints.

Jake returned to the car and told Scott that he would take the wheel for the next couple of hours. Annie had told Jake to stay with the surveillance until she could get another a Case Agent and backup from New York in to cover. She also told Jake that when he was told to break off surveillance at 5pm, that he and his partner make his way to a Philadelphia Airport where there was a private plane to fly them to Miami where they believed the container was heading. He relayed the orders to Scott who could not mask his excitement. At some point, after Scott had sang "Going back to Miami" by the Blues Brothers more times than Jake cared to remember, he threatened to throw Scott out of the car.

The container stopped just south of Philadelphia at a "Truck Only" rest stop. This caused problems for the surveillance team. Orders came over the radio for Car 52 to continue on into the truck stop and to act as if they were having a tire problem. Agent Sandra Kuertz and Agent Gary Eastlund in Car 52 parked up just across from the container. Agent Eastlund took his pocket knife and stabbed the back tire then opened the trunk and took out the spare tire, the tire iron and the jack. Agent Kuertz played a great sympathetic wife, throwing her hands in the air. The truck driver had left his cab door open while he smoked a cigarette. He wandered over to Agent Eastlund,

"Got a flat? Y'all need some help?"

"Hey Man that would be great. My wife here has had four back surgeries so I could really do with a hand" Agent Gary Eastlund replied and held out his hand.

"The name's Joe. I'm driving that piece of shit truck over there, oops sorry Ma'am"

"That's a hell of a truck. I'm Gary. Where are you heading, Joe?"

By this time Joe was already on his knees placing the jack while Gary was loosening the lug nuts.

"Down to the Sunshine State and Miami, if the damn truck makes it that far. What about you?"

"Heading to the wife's mothers house in South Carolina, unless we get another flat."

"We can make that happen" Joe laughed and winked at Sandra.

"Don't be doing that Joe", Sandra said laughing " otherwise, your new buddy will have a hefty taxi bill, because we are going to my Mom's come what may!"

"Shiiit, you're a tough one. Gary, I guess you're going too, if you know what's good for you" Joe cackled.

"I hear you man. How long have you been driving the big rigs?" Joe asked as he tried to shimmy the wheel off.

Joe stood upright, pulled an oily rag from his dungarees pocket and wiped his forehead and nose with it. A black streak was left over his right cheek.

"I was driving big rigs, tractors, trailers since I was about ten. My folks had a farm and we all pitched in. I love being on the road. Away from the wife and kids. Sometimes I'm gone for a week at a time, then others, I have no work. I ain't working for anyone though. I'm my own boss and I like to keep it that way. This job they wanted me to drive their truck instead of mine. It's a piece of shit inside and out. Not my problem. If I don't make it, it's their problem, and, I told them that"

The wheel was off and Joe was already pushing the spare on. Keen to keep the conversation going, Gary asked,

"If you don't mind me asking how much do you get for a job like this?"

"Nope, don't mind. Normally I use my own truck and it's based on miles, weight and the price of diesel. This job was different. They only called me yesterday and they were lucky I had nothing else on. Guess it's a rush job. Got to get this container down to the Miami dockyards to meet a ship. Offered me $5000 to get it there. They pay for fuel, I pay my expenses, couldn't turn it down. Truck's a piece of shit though".

Sandra chirped in,

"So what's in the container? Anything exciting. I've seen pictures of them on the freighters. They look like toy bricks all piled up."

"Papers say I'm carrying medical supplies but have no idea what. The container is locked and I'm not opening it. Just going to get it to Miami and pick up my money".

"Are you going to stay in Miami a little while and catch a few rays" Sandra winked at him

"Hell no, I'm gonna drop the container, pick up my money and drive this piece of shit back to New York. Well, I think your set there. That will get you to South Carolina and Mom's house"

Gary reached into his pocket and pulled out his wallet.

"What do I owe you Joe"

"Hell nothin. Glad to help. Got to get you to Mom's house safely"

"You're a standup guy Joe" Gary reached out and shook his hand again.

"Yeah, thanks so much Joe" Sandra added " I hope you have a safe journey down to Miami".

Joe gave a smile and walked back to his truck lighting up another cigarette. He took three long drags, threw it down and stepped on it. He climbed into his truck and waved as he passed the two of them on his way to the on ramp of I-95.

As he cleared the ramp, Sandra radioed into control and advised Agent Annie Udell what had transpired. Car 52 was given orders to break away from surveillance, return to New York and to document everything that had happened.

Jake and Scott had left the surveillance once the truck had pulled into the rest stop and were pulling into the parking lot at the FBI office at Philadelphia International Airport as Agent Sandra Kuertz radioed into control. They listened to the report and then headed to the terminal to meet the private plane to take them to Miami. It was pouring down as they took a bus across the runway to the opposite side of the airport.

"Make sure you don't cut off any planes" Jake shouted up front to the driver

"Yeah right" the driver yelled back. "What idiot would do that?"

Thunder rumbled across the sky as Scott and Jake ran up the boarding steps to the small twin engined Cessna aircraft.

"Jesus we are going to be like a supermarket cart taking off in this storm" Jake shouted to Scott.

Scott looked as white as a sheet as the engines started and they approached the runway. They sat on the side of runway for what seemed like an eternity as plane after plane took off and landed in front of them, each time causing the Cessna to shake.

"I'm rethinking this whole thing" Scott yelled out to Jake over the noise of the battering rain and the engines.

"Too late" Jake yelled back as the Cessna moved onto the main runway, picked up sped and within seconds was in the air. They lurched back and forward as they encountered air pockets until they rose above the clouds.

"Shit even I need a drink now" Jake said looking peaky himself.

The plane's attendant Carole told her two passengers that they had orders not to serve alcohol on the flight, however, perhaps a small brandy may be needed for medical reasons. She served two very healthy brandies, rendering them both asleep within half an hour.

The Cessna landed at Miami International Airport to bright sunshine and warm temperatures. As soon as the Cessna door was open, the heat permeated the cabin and two agents, refreshed from their brandy influenced drinks, walked down the debarking steps savoring the warm sun on their pale faces.

They were ushered by private car to the customs office where they were briefed on the location of the truck and container as well as more information on the truck driver, Joe Leadbetter. From the intel that had already been researched on Joe, he was a blue-collar worker out of Queens. He was married with two teenaged sons. He had a registered Partnership in the State of New York, "Joe's Trucking". His wife was named as his partner. Mrs. Janet Leadbetter was the office manager and book keeper. Joe did the trucking. No illegal activity was found for the company or for Joe and Janet individually. It seemed Janet had a number infractions and a heavy foot, as all were speeding violations.

Case officer Annie Udell has been relieved by an alternate and she would be arriving in Miami the following morning. A hotel suite had been booked at the Ramada close to the Miami Docks area. Scott and Jake would spend the night at the hotel and would be joined by Annie Udell and other officers the following morning.

Still wide eyed and bushy tailed, after writing up individual reports of the days happening, Scott and Jake decided to hit the hotel bar. For a Monday evening the place was hopping. They found seats at the bar and ordered a round. Jake heard a soft sultry voice behind him,

"Well hello stranger"

Jake spun his bar stool around to see a beautiful black woman in black sleeveless dress which clung to every part of her tall slender body.

"Well hello right back" Jake said as he slid off the stool, took her hand and gently kissed it.

The lady introduced herself as Cheri and sank, very gracefully, onto Jake's bar stool.

"What's your name stranger?" She purred.

"Ted" Jake replied not taking his eyes off her.

"Ted, as in Teddy Bear" Cheri purred back

Scott rolled his eyes, shook his head and looked around to see if Cheri had a friend.

"Who are you with Teddy Bear?" she cocked her head to one side, picked up Jake's drink and sipped it provocatively.

"I'm with my girlfriend, but she's not here right now, and you are" Jake smiled.

Cheri abruptly got up, turned around and walked away.

Jake was flabbergasted, looked at Scott and said,

"What just happened?"

Before Scott could answer, the bar man came over,

"What happened, my friend, was you just saved yourself a hell of a lot of money. Cheri is, let's say, a high-class escort who only drinks the best champagne and will take you for thousands. You did well to mention your girlfriend"

Scott burst out laughing behind Jake and began to sing "My Cheri Amour" by Stevie Wonder. Even Jake saw the funny side and bought the bar man a drink.

By 8am the following morning, the hotel suite looked more like an office with agents milling around everywhere. The couches were pushed to one side and a folding table had been placed in the middle of the floor. A flip chart was off to one side.

"May I have your attention" Annie Udell yelled above the noise and walked towards the flip chart.

"Good morning, everyone find a seat so they can see the flip chart" Annie waited until the noise and rustling of papers had stopped.

"For those not familiar with this case, welcome to Operation Article Frost. We are represented today by DEA, INS and FBI. Later on this morning I will be meeting with the Miami local police, Miami Sheriff and Miami Coastguard. For the past eight months the New York DEA office has been surveilling a container which we believe, through credible intel, contains a large amount of cocaine. The container was located in a Brooklyn dockyard and was under 24 hours surveillance. Yesterday, at approximately 7:30am, the container was picked up by a truck driver and is currently en route to Miami. At this point we do not believe the truck driver, Joe Leadbetter, is criminally involved in Arctic Frost, however he remains a suspect until he is fully cleared.

Our container just crossed the Florida/Georgia border. Florida DEA are now following the container. The Georgia DEA have broken off their pursuit and will submit reports forthwith. We anticipate the container will arrive in Miami around 1pm this afternoon.

From undercover investigations, we believe the truck will deliver the container to a "inland port", which is an off-dock storage yard for empty containers located less than ten miles from the Port of Miami. This warehouse district is easily accessed by Interstate 95 and is a 400-acre facility.

We believe the container will be dropped in the south west corner of the facility. We already have an undercover surveillance crew in place. Once the container is dropped, according to our information, Joe Leadbetter will remain in Miami overnight and then take the truck back to New York to return it to the company who contracted him to do this job. We intend to apprehend Mr. Leadbetter after he has dropped the container and cleared the area. We will bring him in for questioning. At the same time, we will have forensics go over the truck, rig it with tracking devices and audio recording capability. Once we have cleared Mr. Leadbetter, wearing a wire, he will deliver the truck back to New York and return it as scheduled, then we will continue that side of the investigation through our New York office. Does any one have any questions so far?"

"Ok moving on. Once the container is in place, another tracking device will be placed. From intel, we believe that the container will be emptied with 24 hours of it arriving. The cartel we are dealing with have suffered a massive loss in another undercover operation and need to move this cargo quickly. For the first 48 hours we will have full surveillance from all agencies and be ready for take down. It is imperative that all suspects be considered armed and dangerous. If the container is not emptied and moved again, we will follow the container until the lock is broken. At that time everyone will be arrested and separated immediately. They will be taken into custody at the Miami FBI office and questioned. The goal is to move up the chain of distributors to the cartel boss."

An agent from the Florida FBI office raised his hand.

"Could you clarify the amount of cocaine we believe in this container? Also, which cartel are we dealing with?" He asked.

Annie nodded and replied quietly as if someone else was listening in.

"We believe there could be in excess of 10 tons of Colombian Cocaine originating from Medellin, Colombia under Drug Lord Pablo Escobar. Ladies and gentlemen this would be one of the biggest drug seizures we have ever seen and it will not be given up easily. Watch yourself and watch your partner.

Please meet with your case agent for further instructions. Scott and Jake, you come with me to meet local sheriff and police units. We will rendezvous at the Miami FBI building at 10:30am. Be ready"

Scott and Jake grabbed their paperwork and left immediately with Case Agent Annie Udell.

By noon, over 50 more heavily armed agents and police officers were in place in the south west corner of the Inland Port, however, you wouldn't know it.

By noon, it was 90 degrees Fahrenheit, about normal for June in Miami. Everyone waited trying to find a cool area in the warehouses where they still had the eyeball on the container. They were all wearing Kevlar vests which made them even hotter.

At 1:15pm Joe Leadbetter pulled into the Inland Port, passed the paperwork to the gate man and headed to the south west corner of the facility. Two clicks on the radio signified radio silence. The truck slowly moved the container into place and dropped the container into place.Joe jumped out of the cab. Walked around the container. Checked the lock on the door, mopped the sweat off his forehand with the same oily rag the agents had seen earlier and then got back into his cab. He sat for a little while writing on a clipboard. Then he drove away slowly, totally unaware of what was about to happen.

He pulled out of the gate and turned to join I 95 again on the north bound ramp. He moved into the middle lane and continued northbound for another five miles. A Florida State Trooper pulled in behind him with his lights flashing and siren sounding. Joe steered the truck to the side of the freeway, put in his hazard lights and waited for the Trooper to approach.

"Good afternoon Sir, license, registration and paperwork please"

"Can you tell me why you pulled me over?" Joe enquired as he let out an exasperated breath and reached for his clipboard.

"Sir, I will be happy to discuss that with you but for now I just need that paperwork".

" Sure Officer. It's all here and in order" Joe said passing the paperwork through the window.

"Hang tight there Sir, I will be right back"

The Trooper walked back to his car, about the same time another two State Patrol cars pulled up in front of the truck.

Within minutes the Trooper walked back and told Joe that the truck was to be impounded. He then informed Joe that he would need to accompany him to the Trooper's car as the truck would be driven by another officer.

"You shittin me. Jeez" Joe stared at the officer. The officer did not reply and Joe reluctantly, started to gather his things.

"Please leave everything the way it is. Anything that is yours will be returned to you in due course. Please accompany me back to my car."

"Am I under arrest?" Joe questioned as he pulled himself out of the truck.

"Everything will be explained to you in due course" The Trooper opened the rear door of his car and Joe clambered in.

Joe watched as his truck pulled away driven by another plain clothed officer.

"Look I've cooperated and done everything you have asked me to do. I need to know what's going on" Joe becoming more and more exasperated.

"I'm sorry sir, I can't tell you anymore as I don't know anymore. My orders are to bring you in for questioning" the Trooper replied without turning his head.

"What questioning? I've got nothing to be questioned about. This is crazy. I'm calling my wife as soon as I get to where we are going. Where are we going?"

"Sir, please calm down. All will be explained when we get there"

Joe gave up and looked out of the window, not seeing anything but trying to figure out what was happening.

The heat from the hot sun seemed to be cooling around 6pm. Everything around the container seemed quiet. No one was around. The workers had already quit for the night and gate at the front entrance was down. Two clicks were heard on the radio. The agents surveilling the gate signaled that something was happening. Cameras and video cameras documented two teenagers, roughly fourteen years of age, scoot around the gate and enter the area on two bikes. They made their way over to the south west corner riding in circles to see if they could see anyone in the area. After riding around the container a couple of times, one of the kids got off his bike and walked over to the doors of the container and jiggled with the lock. Still locked and secured, he walked around the container and then looked around again. He signaled to his friend the "ok" sign and the rode away, out of the facility under the gate.

Jake spoke to Scott in hushed whispers from a vehicle hidden within one of the warehouses close to the container.

"Obviously counter intelligence for the mutts dealing with the Coke. It looks good for movement tonight. Close your eyes for half an hour. This is going to be an all nighter. Try and get some sleep."

"Sleep! Are you kidding me. I can hear my heart beating in my ear. There is no goddamn way I can sleep. You try it"

"Hey no problem Man" he moved his shoulders to settle in his seat and closed his eyes.

"You want me to wake you when the action starts" Scott questioned.

"No need." Jake yawned, turned his ball cap the wrong way around, put his sunglasses on and reclined into the seat. Within minutes his breathing changed into the rhythmic sound of a gentle snore.

"Jesus, this guy could fall asleep on my mother's clothes line." Scott was almost jealous.

At one in the morning, the synchronized radios all heard the double click signal. Jake's seat creaked as he pulled it to the upright position.

"Morning Sunshine" Scott whispered.

Jake grunted back and picked up his binoculars.

Surveillance outside the gate had seen an Broncho SUV and a Truck Cab approaching the Inland Dock facility. A large Hispanic man holding an automatic rifle jumped out of the passenger side door of the Bronco, looking around he walked under the lighted gate, inserted a key and pushed the gate open. Still looking around, he got back into the Bronco which then drove through the gate with the Truck cab following behind.

They pulled up to the container. The Hispanic man with the automatic rifle jumped out of the Bronco and was followed by two more large Hispanics holding rifles. From the truck cab, two more armed men wearing woolen ski masks, jumped down from the cab. The truck driver remained in place until the first Hispanic man, presumably in charge, beckoned for him to reverse up to the container. The armed men circled the container and checked out the immediate area. There was a loud bang as the truck cab locked onto the container causing all the men to look around to see if anyone had been alerted by the noise. The Hispanic in charge made circling gestures with his finger signaling to the gang that they needed to finish up and get out of there. Everyone assumed their original places in the truck and the Bronco. Within ten minutes of their arrival, they headed out of the gate with the container driving south bound into the night.

As if someone had rung a bell, agents, police and support personnel came running and driving out of the warehouses and surrounding area. Orders were given over the radio to pursue the Bronco and the truck at a distance. A fixed wing was already air bound and out of sight surveilling the convoy as well as agents from the outside perimeter of the facility. Jake and Scott were first out of the gate listening to the fixed wing giving them directions to the vehicles location. Once on I-95, it was easier for the agents to blend into the unbelievable traffic for 1:15 in the morning.

Three exits down, the Bronco and the truck pulled off the freeway. Fixed wing took over again as the area was quiet industrial area made up of multiple warehouses. About a mile off the freeway, the fixed wing reported that the Broncho had stopped at a large gate. The gate opened and the Broncho pulled in through the gate followed by the truck and container. The gate closed slowly behind them. A large garage door to the warehouse opened and revealed more men wearing large gloves. The truck moved as close to the garage door as possible, too tall to get through it.

By this time, Jake and Scott were in the area away from any street lighting, as well as multiple other agents in various vehicles. A helicopter was off in the distance close to the freeway to drown out the familiar hum.

Over the radio, Case Agent Annie Udell advised that they had eyes on the container within the compound. She gave orders for the heavily armed swat team to surround the compound and be ready on her command. Agents were also ordered to take positions around the compound unaware what was happening inside, and to maintain radio silence.

From within the compound, a hive of activity was taking place. A forklift truck moved behind the container as the large Hispanic boss walked out of the warehouse with large bolt cutters. Armed men were circled around the container, all staring at the doors of the container as the boss clamped the bolt cutter around the bolt. With very little effort, the bolt fell off and the boss proceeded to push the bar to open the back doors.

"GO GO GO" the radio blasted.

Swat team, Miami Police, Florida State Troopers and Agents from the FBI, DEA, Immigration and Customs swarmed the compound taking everyone by surprise. The armed suspects aimed their rifles at the invaders, but quickly realized they were outnumbered by the armed swat team and Agents.

A helicopter flew over the scene with a large spotlight illuminating the area. From the helicopter a loud voice could be heard,

"Put your weapons on the ground in front of you. Take two steps backwards and get on the ground. On the ground, on the ground"

The suspects complied as the Agents searched the compound for other suspects. Miami Police cuffed all the suspects and hurried them away, individually, into waiting cars with flashing blue lights. With all the suspects gone, the container which had still not been completely opened, was approached by Case Agent Annie Udell and Jake. A video camera was aimed at the door as it slowly opened making a loud squealing noise.

Everyone looked in.

"Bingo" Jake exclaimed. "You know what boss, I think there may be more than ten tons, look how far it goes back".

" Well lets get it, test it, weigh and label it".

Three and a half hours later, the darks skies turned to a peach pink color and the sun peaked up from below the horizon. The last kilo of cocaine was weighed, labeled and taken into custody. All the numbers were tallied and a total of 20 tons of coke had been labeled and taken into custody. DEA Case Manager Annie Udell, Jake, Scott, the Chief of Miami Police and representatives of the Miami FBI, Immigration and Customs posed for pictures in front of the cache, one of which made front page of the Miami Herald the following day,

"Agents seize 20 tons of Cocaine in raid on Miami Warehouse"

The article went on to talk about the containers travels over the past few days and the fact that the drugs were linked to a Colombian Cartel operating out of Medellin and Cali. Officials had estimated that the wholesale value of the seized cocaine was in excess of two billion dollars, the biggest drug haul in history.

Annie, Jake and Scott reported back to the Miami FBI office where the cocaine, suspects and Joe Leadbetter were being held.

It had been determined that Joe Leadbetter was not involved in the investigation but had agreed to wear a wire when he returned the truck to Brooklyn. During questioning Agents Kuertz and Eastlund walked into the room. The look of bafflement and confusion from Joe was almost comical as he realized that they were part of the whole take down.

"Guess you didn't make it to Mom's house" he directed at Agent Kuertz.

"Actually no," she replied, "but I have to say, such a gentleman I have not met before."

She leaned forward and offered her hand. Joe took it and shook it with a smile breaking out on his face.

"Quite a story for me to tell the Missus" Joe pondered "So are you guys out of New York".

"Yes we are, can I still call you Joe?" Agent Gary Eastlund replied also shaking Joe's hand.

"It's just that the missus is not going to believe a word of this. I may need backup." Joe grinned.

Gary fished a card out of his suit jacket pocket.

"You can reach me or Agent Kuertz on this number. Call us if you have any problems with the missus"

"I sure will Gary, I mean um, Agent....."

"Gary is fine" Agent Eastlund interrupted. "We have to go Agent Kuertz"

As they turned to go, Joe called out

"Hey, did y'all have a flat tire, or was that not real either"

"All part of the cover up Joe, and let's face it, without that, we may have never had a story for you to tell" Agent Kuertz smiled and left the room.

Chapter Five

Jake decided to take a week off work to visit family which he hadn't seen since Christmas. His mother was convinced he had left New York and that she was never going to see him again. The weather had greatly improved and he was ready to visit his old colleagues at the beach.

Jake had began lifeguarding on the beaches of Long Island ever since he had forged his birth certificate at age 15, making him 18 and old enough to take the lifeguard test. As a great swimmer in school, the test was a breeze and from then on he had lifeguarded on Jones Beach and Long Beach, Long Island every summer, except when he was in the military and only on weekends while working with the FBI.

The summer of 1980, could have been one summer that he did not make it to the beach. Jake was sat at his desk in April of 1980, when his phone rang.

"Investigations, Special Agent Taylor speaking"

"Taylor, this is Tony Kuertz, NY Assistant District Director of Investigations. Just heard from Washington. Get a team together, you are going to

Arkansas. You leave in two days, you will be briefed in detail tomorrow"

"What's going on Sir?" Jake replied.

"The God damned Cubans are coming". The phone clicked off and went dead.

Two days later, Jake and twenty of his handpicked fellow agents arrived in Fort Chaffee in Arkansas.

During the late 1970s, Cuba's economy took at sharp downfall. There was mass poverty, no jobs and housing shortages. Cubans began to seek political asylum in the foreign embassies located in Havana, Cuba. Initially Fidel Castro demanded that the asylum seekers be returned to the Cuban Government. When the embassies refused to do this, he reversed his closed emigration policy and declared that those with no revolutionary genes or blood were no longer wanted in Cuba. On April 20th, 1980, Castro announced that anyone wanting to leave Cuba could do so by way of boat from the Mariel Harbor west of Havana.

125,000 Cuban refugees, including those released from prisons and mental health facilities, overwhelmed the US Coastguard over the next five months as 1700 overloaded boats fled to Miami and the US mainland.

Many of the refugees were processed quickly through the immigration camps set up in the Miami area and quickly united with relatives already living in the United States. During this process some of the prisoners released from Cuban prisons were identified and segregated. There was no intelligence from Cuba about any of the refugees. This made the vetting process difficult and extremely challenging. Some refugees were honest about time spent incarcerated, some for stealing a loaf of bread or food for their families. Others with more sinister crimes, in the initial mass chaos, slipped through the vetting process and into American society. Those who were detained with criminal records were transferred to further processing sites in Fort Chaffee, Arkansas, Pennsylvania and Wisconsin.

At the same time Jake arrived in Fort Chaffee, Governor Bill Clinton also mobilized 1000 members of the National Guard believing that Castro agents could be amongst the refugees bound for Fort Chaffee. As area residents began to learn who their new neighbors really were, a mob mentality began to rise. Inadequate security at the Fort gates, refugees with mental health problems and hardened criminals led to a powder keg situation. Although Governor Clinton appealed for calm, it didn't take long before minor demonstrations within the Fort became a full scale riot. 1000 refugees marched towards the gate of the Fort armed with rocks and stones. Shots were fired by the National Guard and chaos ensued. 115 Cubans were arrested, 60 persons were injured and four buildings burned. One of the riot victims, an area resident, stated to a local newspaper,

"It was like war out there"

After the riot, sixty of the worse Cuban agitators were transferred to a Border Patrol Detention Center in El Paso, Texas. Jake lead the team of agents escorting these agitators onto a Braniff Airline flight bound for El Paso. These hardened criminals, shackled by their arms and feet, were shuffled across the tarmac to the awaiting plane. The prisoners were each shackled into seats with one agent to two prisoners. Once all seated the captain demanded to speak with Special Agent Taylor.

"Are you armed Taylor" the captain demanded.

"Yes sir I am" Jake replied.

"Then you are in the cockpit with me".

The flight arrived in El Paso safely and without incident. Once the plane stopped on the tarmac, a double security ring of 30 armed agents converged around the front of the plane while buses drove to the rear of the plane. The prisoners were led two at a time from the plane and onto the waiting buses.

Jake and his team employed many of the locals from the Fort Chaffee area to help with the administration work. Many came from little farming towns and couldn't believe that they were suddenly working with Federal Agents out of Manhattan, New York. As the Agents and their local staff, mainly woman, got to know each other, friendships were formed as they shared stories of their homes and lives. Jake's secretary had never eaten in a restaurant with linen napkins. She had never had a shrimp cocktail. Jake made sure that she experienced both within the first month of meeting her. Jake recalls that after the locals received their first pay check, the woman came back to work the following Monday in new outfits, heels, a new hairdo and manicured nails.

For the Cubans it was even more of a culture shock. When a secretary lit a cigarette with a Bic Lighter, the look of astonishment on the faces of the Cuban refugees was tangible. The flip top on a can of coke was also a thing of great mystery to the refugees. It soon became very clear that not all of the segregated refugees sent to Fort Chaffee were trouble makers. Many were just decent people pushed to the limit by a ruthless leader and terrible circumstances.

As the weather became hot and humid, Jake told his team that they could shed their suits and wear casual, cooler clothing. As more Agents from different parts of the country arrived, the Manhattan team were looked down upon due to their different interpretations of the rules. Eventually, after a number of complaints filed to Washington DC, the Manhattan team were pulled back to New York, just in time for Jake to resume his time on the lifeguard stand, on the weekends, through the summer.

By the time Jake moved from New York to his current home in Florida, he had completed over 45 years of service as a Long Island Ocean Lifeguard. He accumulated many funny, and sometime painful stories over the years. One of his favorites to tell was when he went swimming during a jelly fish invasion on Long Beach. As Jake swam into the surf, a large man o'war jelly fish attached itself to Jake's face with its tentacles in his right eye. He was treated at the hospital and before he left, was interviewed by a news reporter for a local television station. Jake recalled the incident, with a few minor embellishments, to the reporter. He returned to his condo, showered, shaved and went back to the beach to be interviewed by three more news stations. Each interview revealed more alarming details. In one interview Jake described himself as being in "shock", another he was in a fetal position, in another, seizures may have been involved. Fortunately, one of Jake's friends taped all the interviews as they were screened that evening on various tv stations. At many parties, the tape was played to raucous roars of laughter from the partygoers.

There were more serious stories that were also recounted.

One Fourth of July weekend when Jake was off duty from the FBI and was not working that day as a Lifeguard, he decided to go to the beach early for a workout. The beach was already busy with sunbathers crowding the sand. The ocean was calm with boats and jet skis scattered along the waterfront. Jake decided to remain in shallow water due to the amount of boats. He porpoised into the surf and began to swim the length of the beach in about three feet of water. His elbows rhythmically came above the waves as he progressed forward. As he turned to take a breath, he saw the hull of a boat speeding towards him. It was too late for him to escape. He automatically put his right arm up in front of him as the boat hit him rendering him unconscious for a few seconds. He came around to the sound of screams. He was very aware that his right arm had been severely injured as blood mixed with salt water. He looked towards the beach and saw people running and pointing, Jake turned around to see the same boat heading towards him again. This time he fell backwards as the boat sharply turned. Jake's heel was torn from his foot upon impact with the propeller. This time Jake remained conscious and in great pain. He reached out and grabbed his heel as it began to sink. Lifeguards swarmed towards him together with other beach goers. Jake was in and out of consciousness as they brought him back to the beach. He was secured onto a backboard and the lifeguards ran him to the roadway where a medical helicopter was waiting for him.

It was unknown as he went into surgery whether his arm could be saved. After eight long hours Jake came out of surgery with both arms and his heel intact. He could no longer turn his right arm due to nerve damage and he was married to a wheelchair for the next six weeks. The initial investigation into the accident was focused on linking the boat and captain to any FBI cases which Jake had been involved in. The fact that the boat had hit him once, turned and hit him again, made many believe that this was a "hit" on Jake. It was finally determined that the captain had been drinking and was driving recklessly. The investigation also revealed that the young female lifeguard watching that area of the beach, was asleep in her lifeguard chair during the first accident, therefore not sounding an immediate alert which may have stopped the boat hitting Jake for the second time.

As Jake recovered, he realized that he would no longer be able to reload his 357 revolver which all agents had to carry. Facing the loss of his career, fate intervened and the Justice Department changed the carry weapon to a 9mm semi-automatic, which involved inserting a clip into the gun making it possible for Jake to reload. It was two months before Jake could return to work. During his rehab he would go to Church with his mother every Sunday. One Sunday, as the Priest asked the congregation to offer each other the sign of peace. Jake turned to the man in the pew behind him to shake his hand. As he turned, he realized that the man was the captain of the boat which had hit him. As they shook hands, the captain's eyes filled with tears as he whispered how sorry he was.

A more serious incident happened when Jake met a woman called Denise on Long Beach while he was working as a lifeguard. After a few days of her coming to the beach, while Jake was on duty, they became friends. One afternoon, Jake still had three hours to work when Denise asked Jake if he would take her out to dinner. Jake's condo overlooked the beach so he took Denise to the condo and told her to hang out there while he finished his shift on the beach. When he returned to the condo he was feeling unwell. Denise had already consumed a number of beers and insisted they needed to go out to dinner as she had been waiting so long. She had helped herself to one of Jake's white dress shirts out of his closet and was wearing it over her white shorts with a knot one one side making it more fitted. They went out to dinner where Jake ate and drank little as he began to feel sicker. Denise, on the other hand, was drinking and having a great time with all the waiters. After dinner, Denise wanted to go to a club. Jake at first explained that he was really feeling bad, but gave in when Denise said that they would only stay an hour.

Once at the club, all Jake could do was sip soda water and watch Denise as she continued to drink cocktails while dancing with man after man. Eventually the club manager, Chris Stevens came over the Jake and told him that he would have to get her out of the club because she was teasing the men and was about to cause a fight.

They left the club. While the car was being valeted to the front door, Jake visited the men's room to splash cold water on his face. It was obvious by this time that he was running a fever. As he exited the front door, his new Audi 5000 was sat out front with Denise behind the driver's seat. He asked her to move over so he could drive.

"Jesus" she yelled at him through the drivers window, "you can't drink, you can't eat, you can't dance so you definitely can't drive. Get in before I leave you behind" She began to rev the engine.

Not wanting to create more of a scene, Jake got in the passenger seat and began to doze as Denise drove them back to his condo. As Denise maneuvered down the very busy Jericho Turnpike she failed to stop at a red light and plowed through a busy intersection. Jake's car was hit by two other vehicles. Jake's head hit the windshield but he remained conscious. His car was totaled and the police on their way. No one else was hurt. Denise was crying as the police arrived and was begging Jake to do something. Still stunned, Jake approached the officer at the scene as another officer put Denise in handcuffs. He asked the officer for a professional courtesy and to let Denise go. The officer looked at Jake with blood running down his face from a gash on his forehead, felt sorry for him and told the other officer to uncuff Denise. Jake called a buddy who picked them up and drove them to Jake's nephew's home. Jake borrowed a car and took Denise home to Queens. All the way to Queen's,

Denise thanked Jake promising she would make this right and pay for all the damage.

After two days in bed recovering, Jake contacted Denise and was told that she would have nothing to do with the accident and that Jake would have to deal with it. Any further contact would have to go through her lawyer.

Jake contacted his lawyer and relayed the story. Denise's lawyer was contacted. He advised that if Jake was to pursue this case, Denise would say that Jake attacked her in the car causing her to crash.

Weeks passed as Jake dealt with the aftermath. Out of the blue, Denise's lawyer contacted Jake and advised that Denise had received monies from a lawsuit where she had sued a bagel company for a chipped tooth. Denise, obviously feeling some guilt, had told her lawyer to give these monies to Jake to help replace his car. Although well short of the value of his Audi 5000, Jake accepted the funds and learned a valuable lesson.

It was his lifeguarding which caused all of the trouble associated with his posting to the special US Customs task force "Just Say No" against the fight of illegal drugs. This was spearheaded by Nancy Reagan,

America's First Lady in 1984. This was a prestigious position based on Jake's many years of exemplary service. Unfortunately, this also caused much jealousy for a number of Jake's contemporaries.

Even though Jake was already an FBI Special Agent, his security clearance had to be increased due to his work with the First Lady. Background checks were initiated by OPR (Office of Professional Responsibility), specifically Agent Dave Valerio. Valerio was his jealous contemporary and was determined to find a way to stop this promotion from coming to fruition. Jake's family, neighbors and colleagues at the beach were interviewed. At first Valerio presented the case that a position as a lifeguard was beneath that of an FBI agent as well as US Customs Agent. Jake was told that if he wanted to work in this special task force, he would have to leave the beach. Jake begrudgingly was ready to do this until he discovered that President Ronald Reagan had once been a lifeguard in California. He brought this to the attention of OPR, with an accompanying photo of Lifeguard Reagan, further angering Special Agent Valerio.

It seemed that every avenue that Valerio searched to find wrong doing on the part of Jake, he came back empty handed. After the swearing in ceremony, as it seemed imminent for Jake to transfer over to his new position, Valerio became desperate in his efforts to sabotage Jake's career move. He fabricated a charge that Jake had been working as a lifeguard at the beach when Jake had stated he was working for the Federal Government. As a Special Agent with OPR, Valerio did not have to substantiate the charge. He forwarded the allegation to the Southern District US Attorneys office believing that Jake would not be able to prove otherwise.

As months went by after the swearing in ceremony, Jake could not understand why he had not transferred over to the new task force. Others at the ceremony were already fulfilling their new positions. After filing through the Freedom of Information Act, he realized what Valerio was trying to do. He did not understand why but knew enough to realize he had a fight on his hands. The fight was not just to prove the inconsistencies in Valerio's case but to prove his honesty and credibility.

 Valerio began to interview Jake's closest colleagues. Although many stood by Jake, others were mindful of Valerio's powerful position in OPR and confirmed some of the untruthful accusations. Many of Jake's friends within the Bureau now looked away as he walked into the office and Jake was no longer able to trust anyone except his best friend and fellow Special Agent Rick Grozen. As the weeks turned into months, Jake became quite despondent despite Rick trying to keep his spirits up. Jake's health started to deteriorate and his current girlfriend left him.

During this time, Jake received a call from a friend and former part time lifeguard colleague, Paul Penefact. Paul was now the Assistant U.S. Attorney of Nassau County. He told Jake that he could not go into details but that Jake should call the Chief Lifeguard of Long Beach, Steve Kyot as soon as possible. Steve Kyot had been chief since 1980 and had known Jake for over twenty years. Steve told Jake that the "Feds" had been sniffing around and asking questions about Jake. They had interviewed a number of lifeguards insinuating that Jake allegedly had stolen money from the City of Long Beach and the United States Government by working on the beach when he was supposed to be working for the FBI. One of the Captains interviewed by Agent Valerio complained statements had been summarized in a biased manner so providing an impartial version of the interview. The Captain complained to Chief Kyot suggesting that Agent Valerio had been antagonistic, hostile and tried do to put words into his mouth. He stated that the entire demeanor was less than even handed. Another lifeguard came forward and said that his statements had also been misconstrued and the interviewing agent had documented things that he had never said.

Steve also told Jake that he had sworn affidavits from all of the lifeguards disputing the statements written by the interviewing agents.

Jake was speechless, thanked Steve Kyot and requested he send copies of the affidavits to his home address. As he hung up the phone, he felt a sudden wave of nausea which brought him to his knees. Although grateful to know that his fellow lifeguards had his back, Jake became increasingly depressed and despondent.

Although Jake had tried to prove his innocence through official documentation he had submitted surrounding his surveillance and arrests, Valerio's always found a way of disputing the facts. Jake felt that there was no way out, even though he had so many exemplary letters of recognition from all the agencies he had worked alongside since his swearing in as an FBI Special Agent.

Depressed, feeling very alone and desperate, Jake realized he needed an attorney. He had no idea who to hire. Most of the attorneys he worked with were criminal attorneys representing people he had arrested. He remembered that his friend Tom, a fellow agent who had been his roommate during their time at the FBI academy in Georgia, had been dealing with internal affairs over a corrupt agent. He called Tom who recommended an "up and coming" attorney Roger Aparrone. Tom told Jake that Roger did not come cheap. Jake called Roger Aparrone and was able to retain him using every penny from his savings. Roger listened as Jake outlined the case, Roger became skeptical believing some of what Jake described had been embellished. It was decided that Roger would contact OPR and request a meeting between himself, the US Attorney and Agent Valerio. It was decided that on this occasion, Jake would not attend.

Roger met Agent Valerio and Assistant US Attorney (AUSA) Meg Harper. During this meeting Roger was apprised of the nature of allegations against Jake, namely working for the US Government and lifeguarding at Long Beach simultaneously therefore committing theft from both parties. Both the AUSA and Agent Valerio stated there were no records to substantiate activities of Agent Taylor on any of the dates that he was supposed to be working for the government, therefore they believed he was working at the beach. Agent Valerio advised Roger that he would be very interested in seeing any documentation which would substantiate Agent Taylor's activities. Roger had the feeling this invitation to provide documentation, was basically telling him that, rather than the government furthering their inquiries, Roger would have to do it. Essentially, he was witnessing a role reversal of innocent until proven guilty.

Roger summoned Jake to his office and recounted the meeting between the parties. For the first time, Roger began to believe Jake and the preposterous story he had described at their first meeting. Roger told Jake that they would have to find proof that Jake was actually working for the FBI when he was on the clock.

Jake stood up and announced that he would return the following day at lunch time. Roger agreed and began to ask another question, as he did so, Jake turned and walked out the office door. Roger scratched his head. This case was becoming more bizarre every minute.

The following day, at lunch time, Jake was ushered unto Roger Aparrone's office carrying a large box. He set the box on Roger's desk and indicated for Roger to take a look.

Very quickly Roger realized that this was absolute proof that on the days that Valerio had stated Jake was working on the beach, Jake was actually working as a Special Agent. Jake had supplied Roger with his personal diaries showing exactly what he was doing on those dates on which Valerio had accused him of "double dipping" The diaries confirmed that Jake had been involved with arresting or other legitimate FBI work. This was then confirmed with internal copies of memos between Jake and his superiors, all time and date stamped absolutely exonerating Jake. Jake's demeanor changed and he became anxious to move forward and clear his name.

That same day, Roger Aparrone requested a meeting at with the Assistant US Attorney at the court house in Manhattan. The meeting was set the following week. Jake arranged to meet Roger in the lobby.

The morning of the meeting was hot and humid. Jake took the Long Island Bullet train into Manhattan to avoid the chance of being held up in traffic. His stomach was in knots by the time he got to the Federal Building. He walked to his office. Not one person lifted a head to greet him with a "Good morning". Jake felt so alone. He had always been such a popular guy. This silent treatment was alien to him.

Sick to his stomach, Jake tried to work on his case load but kept looking at the clock. At 10:30am, he left the office and walked across the street towards the

Court Building. On route, he passed St Andrew's Catholic Church. Making a detour, he entered the church and sat in the last pew. The church was dimly lit but the sun streamed through the colorful stained-glass windows. He could smell the burning incense and felt very comfortable. He knelt at the pew, bowed his head and silently prayed for strength. After a few moments Jake stood up, made the sign of the cross and walked out into the bright sunlight. It took his eyes a few moments to adjust. Just as he was able to focus, Roger approached him and patted Jake on the back. In silence, the two of them walked the final 200 yards to the court house.

Roger left Jake in the lobby and went to seek out the Assistant US Attorney Sally Johnson. The court house was very familiar to Jake. He was there often bringing a prisoner in for arraignment or meeting with the judge for a warrant. This was the first time he had sat in the lobby. He looked around to see clients with their attorneys talking to each other in whispered voices. Jake felt like a criminal as he watched the "charged" walk into the court rooms. One lady sobbed as she waited, her attorney periodically passing her tissues.

Roger returned to the lobby with a somber look on his face. He explained to Jake that Valerio was present in the Assistant US Attorney's office. He advised that

Valerio had stated that Jake was under investigation with impending charges, therefore he would not be permitted into the US Attorney's office. This was quite common practice when a citizen was under arrest. The legal counsel would plea on behalf of the accused, while the accused sat in the lobby and waited. Jake was speechless. He would not have the chance to speak and was reduced to that of a criminal sat on a bench. The only difference Jake was not wearing handcuffs.

Roger assured Jake that he believed his evidence was enough and for Jake to trust him. Roger walked away as Jake held his head in his hands. How had this happened? Yes, at times he pushed the envelope with the rules, used the government car on personal business, but for things to come to this! His health was suffering, recently diagnosed with diverticulitis from stress and his normal upbeat demeanor had been replaced with a somber depression.

Attorney Sally Johnson's office was on the second floor. Her office window overlooked Foley Square where people were sat on benches chatting or just relaxing in the sunshine. Pigeons were gathered around those eating hoping for the odd crumb to fall. Sally Johnson was sat at her desk in front of the large window. She was a popular Judge and deemed fair. She looked to be in her mid-fifties, a mousy blond and impeccably dressed. Valerio sat to her right and wore a smirk on his face.

Attorney Aparrone, walked to the rear of the room and retrieved a large three-legged easel holding a flip board. He reached into his brief case and placed six sheets of paper on top of each other onto the stand. The first and top sheet was blank.

He returned to the last empty seat at the desk, hooked his jacket over the back of it and finally sat down.

"Good afternoon, Attorney Johnson, Special Agent Valerio" Roger bellowed. "As you are aware, I am legal counsel for Special Agent Jake Taylor. I have requested this meeting to present evidence in the investigation of my client headed up by the Office of Professional Responsibility and specifically you, Special Agent Valerio"

He turned and faced Valerio who responded,

"I can confirm that charges are imminent Attorney Aparrone"

"Before I begin, Special Agent Valerio, can you explain the basis of your investigation into my client?"

Valerio cleared his voice,

"Your Client, Attorney Aparrone, has been stealing from the State of New York"

"I'm sure you forgot the word "allegedly" in that sentence Special Agent"

Attorney Johnson spoke for the first time,

"Go on Agent Valerio"

"Your client, allegedly, while working for the FBI, on a number of dates, collected his salary when in actuality he was working as a Lifeguard on Long Island, effectively double dipping."

Attorney Aparrone opened his briefcase and took out a notepad and pen,

"Please could you give me the dates in question."

Without saying a word, Valerio, thrust a piece of legal paper across the desk at Roger.

With a smile Roger picked up the paper and read aloud the five dates printed. He then stood up and walked to the easel and flipped the first page over.

"Let's look at these dates, one at a time shall we?"

On the easel was a blown-up copy of a page out of Jake's personal diary.

"From my chart, you see a copy of Special Agents personal diary. As you can see, Special Agent Taylor was involved in the arresting of Carlos Riviera on that date therefore he could not have been working as a lifeguard that day"

Valerio, jumped up from his seat,

"Do you think we are stupid Attorney Aparrone. This is insulting to both myself and Attorney Johnson. You are wasting all our time. These so-called diaries could have been written at any time. He's got you really suckered in; I propose we terminate this meeting right now".

Roger faced Attorney Johnson,

"Attorney Johnson, I would like to give you a document which is date and time stamped. The official FBI document is written by Special Agent Taylor and is addressed to his first line supervisor William Canery. The document outlines the arrest of Carlos Riveria"

Roger calmly walked over to his brief case and pulled at a document and passed it to Attorney Johnson. Valerio leered at Roger as Attorney Johnson inspected the document.

"This is very interesting Attorney Aparrone. Do you have anything else to add?"

Roger flipped the next page of his chart to reveal the second date which, allegedly, Jake had stolen from New York State. This blown-up page of Jake's diary revealed that Jake and his partner were involved in the surveillance of two individuals in the "diamond district" of New York believed to be dealing cocaine. Once again Roger walked to his briefcase and produced an official FBI document date and time stamped from Jake's supervisor William Canery outlining Jake's surveillance and the future plans for the take down of these individuals. He passed the paperwork to Attorney Johnson who glanced at it and then looked back up at Roger,

"Attorney Aparrone, do you have written evidence for the further three dates included in Agent Valerio's investigation?"

"Yes, I do Ma'am"

Attorney Johnson turned to Special Agent Valerio,

"Agent Valerio, have you seen these documents before"

"No Attorney Johnson. They have to be counterfeit".

"I can assure Ma'am that you can also procure these documents from the official FBI files" Roger interjected.

"Yes, I believe you Attorney Aparrone. My question to you Agent Valerio is, if Attorney Aparrone has a copy of these documents, why do you not have one? Did you not tell me, in our last conversation, such documents do not exist?"

Attorney Johnson glared at Agent Valerio waiting for an answer.

Agent Valerio stuttered

"Well" then stopped and shrugged his shoulders.

"Agent Valerio" Attorney Johnson continued, "I have to say that I agree with your earlier statement. This meeting will be terminated. Attorney Aparrone, please advise your client that this investigation stops now. You have proven your case and Special Agent Taylor is completely exonerated from these accusations. Special Agent Valerio will confirm this in writing to Agent Taylor together with an apology. Agent Valerio will also explain to this attorney why I was told that such documentation brought before me today, did not exist".

Agent Valerio, still standing, slumped back into his chair as Attorney Aparrone shook Attorney Johnson's hand, collected his briefcase and paperwork from the easel and left the office.

Jake was no longer sitting on the bench in the lobby. Roger found him outside in the square pacing up and down. Roger walked towards Jake,

"It's over. Let me buy you a drink and I'll tell you everything that happened"

Jake speechless, just followed Roger into a local bar,

"Scotch please, neat" were the first words Jake uttered.

Chapter Six

Jake returned to the Garden City Office refreshed and ready to work again. The past weekend, Jake had received a call from a lifeguard buddy, Larry Mitchell, a New York City Police officer. Larry had told him that the New York Police Summer Olympics were taking place the following week and that he should consider participating. Jake put in papers to request time off and approval to participate. After what had transpired with Valerio, he doubted very much that his request be approved.

The following day, he received notice that not only had this been approved but that he would be receiving a stipend for travel, food and lodging expenses.

The day that he was to travel to upstate New York for the olympics, a large oriental cargo ship ran aground in Brooklyn. The ship was carrying 286 oriental illegal aliens and 13 crew. Within minutes of running aground, 299 occupants fled the ship, a few drowning in the process, and were seen running down streets and highways to escape and avoid capture. Everyone in NY law enforcement, federal and state were told to report to work immediately to deal with this crisis.

Jake called in expecting to be told to come in to the office but was told that he was on a special assignment and to continue to the Olympics.

Jake participated in the swimming races. Each day, another heat was held, all of which he won. On the final day he had a final in every stroke, breaststroke, freestyle, butterfly, backstroke and long distance 1500 meters. By the end of the day, he had won every race and was the proud recipient of five gold medals, a Police Olympic first for any sport.

He returned to the Garden City office a hero! His office was filled with balloons and Jake appreciated the effort that his coworkers had made. This would never have happened in the Manhattan office. After the celebrations, Jake's supervisor, Ted Caturo called him into his office. He told Jake that the Garden City Office were preparing to do a sting operation on smoke shops on Atlantic Avenue in Brooklyn. Jake had missed the briefing last week so Ted caught him up on the details. A few agents are detailed over from the FBI office in Manhattan. You will partner with Rick Grozen. I think you may know him.

"Rick is a good friend of mine. We have worked together many times. He's a good guy".

"Yes Rick was briefed last week, he'll get you up to par with it all. He should be here soon". Ted advised.

Jake walked out of Ted Caturo's office.

"Howdy partner" Rick yelled across the office, walked over and gave Jake a big bear hug.

"Just like old times, partner. Starsky and Hutch ride again" Jake smiled. It was good to see his old friend again.

Smoke Shops could be found up and down Atlantic Avenue. The shops were made to look like "Mom and Pop" stores but were run by mostly black Jamaican Rastafarians to sell marijuana. When you entered this store there was metal wall with a cut out window for customers to place their orders. A tray would be slid out of the window for the customer to place the money on and then the marijuana would be sent out on another tray. It was almost like doing a transaction at a bank but a little more seedy!

The first smoke shop, they had received intel that the owner had a Tec-9 powerful handgun. Jake and Rick walked into the store. It was empty of customers. Jake went to the door at the end of the wall and pushed it open shouting that this was a raid by the

FBI. At the same time Rick banged on the metal wall to distract the teller. A lone tall Rastafarian met Jake,

"On the ground, on the ground, lie flat with your arms above your head" Jake yelled. His voice echoed around the metal wall making it sound as if there were multiple agents in the raid. Jake handcuffed his hands behind his back and then assisted the guy to his feet.

"You're under arrest. Where's the gun?" Jake yelled

"I have no gun man" the prisoner yelled back

"Where's the gun, where's the gun?" Jake yelled again

"No gun man, I swear man"

In the corner Jake saw a baseball bat. He told Rick to get it. Jake kicked a stool closer to his prisoner.

"Put your leg up on the stool" Jake yelled

His prisoner complied,

"What you doing man?" he yelled.

Jake calmly replied "I'm going break your leg unless you give up the gun"

"Wait" the Rastafarian yelled, taking his foot off the stool "Break this one instead" and placed his other leg on the stool.

Jake was dumbfounded. He didn't expect that answer. He was never going to break the guy's leg. He told the guy to sit on the stool while Rick searched the back area for the gun and found nothing. They were just about to take their prisoner out to the government car, when the bell from the front door rang. Jake put his finger over his lips to indicate to everyone not to speak. Rick held onto their prisoner. Jake spoke through the window,

"Hey Man, what you need?"

A white kid, around 17 years old replied,

"Who are you? You're not the usual guy."

"Man, stop wasting my time. What do you want?" Jake yelled.

The kid made his order and reached to put his money on the tray, Jake immediately slapped a pair of handcuffs around his wrists.

"What's a young kid like you doing here buying marijuana?" Jake walked around the wall to see that the kids had quite obviously urinated on himself.

"I'm going up to the Hamptons this weekend with my buddy."

Jake looked outside the store and saw the kids buddy in the passenger seat of a red BMW.

He uncuffed the kid.

"Get out of here and don't let me see you down here again, or I will arrest you next time."

The kid didn't wait to be told again and bolted out of the store.

Jake radioed for the backup to clear the store of drugs and put the Rastafarian in the car to take him in for processing.

As they drove west down Atlantic Avenue, Jake saw the red BMW outside another known smoke shop and rolled his eyes. He couldn't stop as they already had prisoner in the car.

They took their prisoner to 26 Federal Plaza to process him. Jake realized he had left his wallet in the car and walked down to the garage to retrieve it. He met another agent coming from his car. He had his suit coat wrapped around his wrist.

"Hey Donnie, Everything ok?" Jake inquired.

"Shit no, I punched some guy and broke my wrist. Not sure how this is going to go down" Donnie answered.

Jake thought for a minute.

"Where's the guy you punched?"

"I let him go" Donnie admitted.

"Donnie, where's your car? Does it have a spare tire?"

"Yes, the car's parked on the back wall"

"Come on, let's go" Jake started to walk towards the car.

Jake jacked the car up and removed the tire. He took the new tire out of the trunk, quickly turned and smashed Donnie in the chest with the tire and pushed him into the wall.

"Jesus, What the hell." Donnie yelled

"Listen, you had a flat, you jacked up the car to put a new tire on, the jack slipped and hit you in the wrist. That's how you broke it".

Jake walked away, retrieved his wallet and joined Donnie at to the elevator.

"I owe you one Jake" Donnie smiled.

Jake nodded his head and went to find Rick.

The following day, they had a lead on a Jamaican selling drugs out of his apartment in the Bronx. Rick and Jake knocked on the apartment door and were met by Jamaican man dressed only in his underwear.

"Is there anyone else in the apartment" Jake asked him as he could hear water running.

"Nah man, just me" he replied.

Jake walked up the hallway and opened the bathroom door. A shower curtain was closed and the shower was running. Jake pulled the curtain back to reveal a gorgeous tall blonde German woman who appropriately screamed and used some unknown German profanities.

The Jamaican was arrested and taken in to Manhattan for processing. Back at the office in Garden City, Jake started talking about the woman in the shower. He couldn't understand how such a beautiful woman could end up with a drug pushing low life.

"Drugs, my friend" Rick replied. "Most of these women are flight attendants who are in the city on a layover"

"Perhaps I'm in the wrong business" Jake mused as they left together to go home.

That weekend, Jake arranged to meet his friend Janice in Manhattan for dinner. It was late by the time they left the restaurant and they were deep in conversation as they walked down 6th Avenue. As they approached 58th Street, Jake stopped suddenly, yelled at Janice to call 911 and took off running towards a parked car across the street. A woman in the front seat, was being mugged by two attackers. As Jake pulled off one of the assailants, both fled the scene with Jake in pursuit. Although armed, Jake did not use a weapon and was able to apprehend one of the assailants. As he turned to face the assailant he realized she was a woman with a short crew cut. He restrained her until, the police arrived.

The woman was a prominent business owner in Manhattan and owned the building 100 Central Park South. She wrote to the FBI requesting that a meritorious award be awarded to Jake. He was called back to the FBI office to be presented with a Special Achievement Award. Afterwards he was called into Valerio's office to be admonished and to be told that he was not a policeman and not to conduct himself in that way ever again.

Monday morning, Jake had a note on his desk to meet Ted in the conference room at 9am. He knocked on the door and entered the large conference room. The oak table was loaded with files and papers. Ted, the only occupant, sat at the head of the table. He welcomed Jake with a smile and beckoned for him to sit down. Ted reviewed with Jake the meetings between the US Attorney, Anthony Morgan, Michael Stein and his counsel Benjamin Pello. He handed a file to Jake and told him to find somewhere quiet to read the agreement they had filed.

The letter was addressed to Ben Pello. It read,

"Re: United States v. Michael Stein 87-367M

This letter is being written to confirm the agreement entered into between this office and your client, above captioned case.

It is agreed in exchange for the promises set forth below, that your clients will cooperate fully with this office, agents of the Federal Bureau of Investigation, FBI, The immigration and naturalization service, INS, the drug enforcement administration, DEA and all the law enforcement agencies as this office may require. This cooperation will include the following:

1. *Mr. Stein agrees to be fully debriefed concerning his knowledge of, and participation in, all his prior criminal activity, included but not limited to drug trafficking and bribery of INS officials. This debriefing will be conducted by this office, agents of the FBI, the DEA, INS and other law-enforcement agencies as this office may require.*

All documents which are relevant to the investigation and which are in Mr. Stein possession or under his control will be furnished to this office upon request. All information provided by Mr. Stein shall be truthful complete and accurate;

2. *Mr. Stein agrees to testify as a witness before a grand jury in this district or elsewhere as may be requested, and any results in trials, either in this district or elsewhere, as this office may require.*

3. *Mr. Stein agrees to cooperate with agents of the FBI, the DEA, the INS and all that law enforcement agencies, as this office may require, and investigations arising from information provided by him. This cooperation includes, but is not limited to, undercover introductions; and*

4. *Mr. Stein agrees to testify, as this office may require, either by way of deposition, letters, oratory, by personal appearance or other means, or before any foreign courts or tribunal. In exchange for the cooperation of Mr. Stein as set out above, this office agrees to the following.*

5. *This office will permit Mr. Stein to plead guilty to a felony information charging him with one count of conspiring to bribe an INS official in violation to title 18, United States code, section 367, to cover heretofore disclosed participation in any criminal activity involving the bribery of an INS official and the distribution of cocaine. Such participation*

includes Mr. Stein involvement in (1) the making of various bribery payments to an undercover INS agent, and (2) the distribution of Cocaine to an undercover INS agent on three occasions, all such activity taking place in the Eastern District of New York between January 31, 1986 and May 27, 1987. Mr. Stein agrees that this plea of guilty will be taken under oath pursuant to Rule 11(c) (5). Furthermore, no information so disclosed by Mr. Stein during the course of his cooperation will be used against him.

6. *This office, prior to Mr. Stein's sentencing, will advise the sentencing court of the nature and extent of his cooperation including its investigative and prosecutive value, truthfulness, completeness and accuracy. In this connection it is understood that this office's determination of the value, truthfulness, completeness and accuracy of this cooperation shall be binding upon the defendant and its statement to the sentencing court may be made either orally or in writing. However, this office will make no specific recommendations with respect to sentencing. This office makes no representations to Mr. Stein concerning any sentence that may be imposed upon the aforementioned plea of guilty, such matters being solely within the province of the sentencing court.*

7. *This agreement is limited to the United States Attorney's office for the Eastern District of New*

York and cannot bind any federal state or local prosecuting authorities.

It is further understood that Mr. Stein must at all times give complete, truthful and accurate information and testimony. Should it be judged by this office that Mr. Stein has intentionally given false, misleading or incomplete information or testimony or has otherwise violated any provision of this agreement, this agreement may be deemed null and void by this office and Mr. Stein will thereafter be subject to prosecution for any federal criminal violation of which this office has knowledge, including but not limited to perjury and obstruction of justice. Any such prosecution may be premised upon any

information provided by Mr. Stein during the course of his cooperation and such information may be used against him. Also any previously entered plea will stand.

Finally, it is understood that this agreement was reached without regard to any civil tax matters that may be pending or may arise involving Mr. Stein.

It is further agreed that if the Mr. Stein requests, and in our judgment the request is reasonable, we will make application and recommend that he be placed in the "witness protection program", it being understood that the United States attorney only has authority to recommend, with the final decision to *place him in the program rests with the Department of Justice, who will make such a decision in accordance with applicable departmental regulations.*

No additional promises, agreements and conditions have been entered into other than those set forth in this letter and none will be entered into unless in writing and signed by all parties

If the foregoing accurately reflects the agreement entered into between this office and your client.

Michael Stein, it is requested that he and yourself execute this letter as provided below.

Sincerely
Anthony Morgan
United States Attorney

At the bottom of the letter the following was written and signed by Michael Stein.

I have received this letter from Assistant United States Attorney Anthony Morgan, and discussed it with my attorney Benjamin Pello, Esq, have read it,

and I hereby acknowledge that it fully sets forth my
agreements with the office of the United States
Attorney's for the Eastern District of New York. I state
that there have been no additional promises or
representations made to me by any officials of the
United States Government in connection with this
case.

Mike Stein

Michael Stein

Witnessed by;
Counsel for the defendant.

Ben Pello

Benjamin Pello Esq

After reviewing the agreement, Jake walked back in to
Ted's office and placed the agreement onto his desk.

"I think everything is covered in the agreement, but
Stein will not go for the Witness Protection Program, I
don't think his wife would agree to it."

"There have been more developments with Stein,
Jake. We are baffled by this but I guess the guy still
likes you after the undercover operation. He has

agreed to all elements covered in the agreement, however, he wants to continue to work with you, undercover, until we arrest Bob Branson".

Jake thought for a moment,

"I can't believe that Stein still trusts me, however it does makes sense. I know all the players and Branson knows me from the most recent sales with Tania."

"That's another thing" Ted answered, "he never wants to see Tania again!"

"Figures" Jake said. "Where is Stein now?"

"He's back working at the car wash. He's real scared Jake. You should set up a meeting with him but wear a wire each time. I also spoke to your superiors in Manhattan. We've already come to an agreement to extend your detail"

"Got it Sir"

Jake got up and left the office. In a way, he felt good about the fact that Stein wanted to work with him. An odd type of friendship had been forged between the two of them, even though Jake had been undercover the entire time. Jake felt more control knowing he would be working with Stein again. He also thought he could protect him in some way.

That afternoon, the 6th of August, 1987, Jake met Stein at the car wash. He looked around for Stein's wife, Diana. Instinctively Stein quietly mumbled,

"She's staying with her mother. She doesn't want anything to do with this deal with Branson. She's scared Jake"

Jake replied,

"I know man. She's safer there but, we have to do this right so no one gets hurt. We only need to make two buys from Branson and we're done"

Stein, usually loud and cocky, remained subdued and quiet as the two of them spoke and formulated a plan. Stein would call Branson later in the week and tell him that Jake wanted eight ounces of cocaine for $15,000. He would also tell Branson that Jake needed the coke by August 24th. Jake would return to the car wash before Stein made the call, to set up a phone tap.

Although, extremely nervous, Stein did a great job, cajoling with Branson over the phone. Stein indicated that he did not know what Jake was going to do with the cocaine which immediately led to Branson asking more questions. Stein brushed off any impropriety by indicating that Jake was always reliable and on time with the money and that he hadn't caused any problems.

Late on August 19th, Stein called Jake at home and told him that Branson had just called him and said Jake would have to wait until September 4th for the cocaine. It was obvious to Stein, Branson wanted to test Jake and let him know that he called the shots.

They arranged to meet the following day at Potter Park in Rockville Center so Jake could document what he had just heard and for Stein to sign the statement. He told Stein to call back Branson to tell him that Jake was not happy and that Stein had told him to take it or leave it.

On September 4th, as agreed, Jake met Stein at the car wash with $15,000 in large bills. Stein had been under surveillance since his arrest. He obviously didn't know it or Jake would have been the first to know. Jake had toyed with telling Stein that he would have a team following him to Branson's house, however after seeing how nervous he was, he decided not to. Jake made arrangements to meet at Potter Park at 6pm that same evening.

At 5:30pm, Jake had received word from the agents surveilling Stein, that he was still at the residence of Bob Branson. He asked the agents to page him as soon as Stein left the home.

For the first time since his undercover had begun almost two years ago, Jake began to worry. If Branson had broken Stein, he would undoubtedly end Stein's life, and probably go after his wife also. It would be difficult to bring Branson up on charges, the evidence was all circumstantial.

Suddenly, Jake's pager went off and he received word that Stein's car had just left the home of Branson. He asked for verification from the surveillance team that it was actually Stein driving in the car and that he was alone. Confirmation followed quickly and everything was back on track.

Jake felt physically sick as he entered the parking lot of Potter Park at 7pm. Within five minutes, Stein pulled in behind. Jake requested that the surveillance team stay hidden and he beckoned Stein to join him in his government car.

Stein looked ill. He had lost weight since his arrest and dark circles encompassed his eyes.

"How did it go Mike?" Jake asked with obvious empathy in his voice.

"Fuckin terrible. Branson asked me a bunch of stupid questions, I thought he knew Jake, I thought I would not get out of that place alive. He took a call while I was there. Whoever it was took his attention, he walked out of the kitchen and I waited for almost an hour for him to come back. When he did, he said he had to leave, gave me the coke and I left. I can't do that again, Jake, we gotta find another way".

"I'm sorry Mike but this is the only way. We have to do it one more time. I'll call you tomorrow and we will set up another buy."

Stein, defeated, got out of the passenger door, with slumped shoulders he got back into his car and drove away slowly.

Jake returned to the Garden City Office and met with the surveillance team as well his back up team, Lemar and Sands. The cocaine was taken into evidence and each team member documented their part in that evening's activities.

It was midnight before Jake got home. He was exhausted both emotionally and physically. It had been a rough day. As much as he wanted Branson, he did not want to Stein to get hurt. He needed to keep Stein as calm as he could and get the next buy planned quickly.

At the Garden City Office, everyone included in Adonis met in the conference room. Jake's superior from the FBI office, Assistant Special Agent in Charge (ASAC) William Canery , Tania with her superior from DEA, two supervisors from INS, Lemar and Sands sat around the large white table. Ted Caturo introduced everyone and gave a short speech on everything that had transpired since the inception of Adonis in January 1986.

Jake then continued advising the next steps which would lead to the arrest of Bob Branson. Then indictments would be processed for Lorenzo Endario, Jusieppi D'Abrevio and the Israelis who had obtained Alien Registration Cards throughout the operation. Jake would coordinate the next buy from Branson then approach the US Attorney for the arrest of Branson. Jake would then arrest Branson and take him into custody. Once Branson was arraigned warrants would be sort for the Israelis, Endario and D'Abrevio. Jake would be the arresting officer in all the cases but would turn the defendants over to INS for arraignment. Stein would plead guilty to a felony charge of bribing an INS agent with the court being made aware that he remained a cooperating witness.

The meeting formally ended but everyone hung around and chatted about different aspects of the case. ASAC Canery walked over to Jake and shook his hand.

"Good work Taylor. There's a commendation waiting for you if this all goes to plan"

"Thank you Sir" Jake smiled, knowing that he had too many enemies in the Manhattan FBI office to allow him a commendation. "Now if you can excuse me…."

"Absolutely" ASAC Canery walked away as Jake left the conference room and placed a call into Stein. They agreed to meet the following week at the car wash.

That weekend, Jake had planned on attending a wedding with a female attorney he had met at 26 Federal Plaza when she was filing for an alien registration card for her client. They had got talking and hit it off immediately. She told him that her client was getting married over the weekend and that she needed to be there to certify the wedding was legal. Jake had asked her if she needed "back up" certification, that he would be happy to accompany her on such a daunting task.

The wedding was at a chic apartment on 5th Ave, Manhattan. It was fully catered by a well known New York chef and hostesses made sure you always had a drink in your hand. The apartment was beautifully decorated in lace and white flowers. Dazzling white chairs were set up in the main room, the white carpeted aisle dotted with red rose petals.

A bell was rung indicating it was time for the wedding. Photographers made their way to the white arch to wait, with the groom and his best man, for the bride to arrive.

A flutist began to play as the bride slowly walked down the aisle alone. She reached the groom, the two of them turned to face the pastor and then, the most bizarre thing happened. The best man tapped the bride on the shoulder, she turned, gave the best man her bouquet and the bride stood to one side. The groom and best man turned to the pastor who began the service.

Quickly it dawned on Jake. Not only was this a marriage of convenience but was a marriage between two men. He looked at Lynne who obviously knew what was going on. He whispered in her ear,

"I can't be here, this is fraudulent. Jesus, you may have told me Lynne."

Jake stood up quietly and made a quick exit. Lynne didn't budge and that was the end of that beautiful relationship!

The final buy from Branson was finally approved by upper echelon of the FBI and DEA. Jake, Lemar and Sands met at the car wash at 4pm on October 30th, to fit Stein with a wire. He'd refused to wear one at the last meet due to fear of Branson finding it. This time Stein had a terrible cold and seemed to think that Branson would not come close enough to him for fear of catching his cold.

He called Branson at his residence at 6pm, as arranged to let Branson know he was on his way. There was no reply. He tried him at the Six Towns Car Wash which was owned by Branson, but was told he was not there. At 6:30pm Stein called Branson's residence again, with no reply. By this time Stein was so stressed, the wire had to be removed as he was sweating so profusely, the sticky patches had detached from his skin.

Jake pulled Lemar and Sands to one side.

"I think we put a stop to this buy tonight. Stein is not going to be able to do it. He's sick to start with and with all this stress he could blow the whole thing."

With Lemar and Sands in agreement, Jake put a call into Ted Caturo. Ted was annoyed that so many people were involved in this meet, including surveillance who were hidden in a car out of sight of the car wash. He also realized that they were so close he didn't want to jeopardize the entire Adonis operation.

"Go ahead, cancel. Have Stein keep trying Branson and give Branson some excuse why he can't go later".

Jake walked into Stein's office where he found Stein sat at his desk with his head leaning on the desk.

"We're going to pull the plug on this tonight. We have to come up with an excuse why you can't go to his residence later if he asks".

"That's easy" croaked Stein. "I'll tell him I'm sick. He's a germaphobic, he will insist I don't go"

"Go home man, call me in the morning" Jake patted Stein on the back "Make sure you document anything Branson says to you if you get through to him"

Stein lifted his head up and then closed his eyes and put his head back on the desk.

Jake called off the surveillance and returned to the office to deposit $4000 back into the INS safe.

When he got back to the condo, he had a message from Stein.

"Jake, this is Mike. I spoke with Branson at 9:30pm. He does not want to see me until I am feeling better. I've set up the next meet for 9pm on November 2nd. The cocaine is at his residence already. Don't call me back tonight, I'm too sick. I'll call you in the morning if I make it through the night. Click"

Nerves were all on edge as Stein was fitted with a wire again on November 2nd. The weather was atrocious. It had rained for the past three days and everyone seemed to be as miserable as the weather.

This time Stein was not required to make a call to Branson, he just needed to be at his residence in Port Washington at 9:00pm. Stein was still sniffling from his cold. Jake guessed Branson would still not get to close to Stein as he was still having symptoms.

Stein pulled out of the car wash at 8pm. Discreetly, a black sedan pulled in behind him to follow him to the destination. Jake returned to the Garden City Office where Ted Caturo waited for him. Ted was in the radio room listening to Stein's wire.

"Jesus Jake. Your guy has done nothing but blow his nose and hack like an old man, since the tap went live. It's pretty disgusting."

"No, it's a good thing Sir" and Jake explained Branson's fear of germs.

"I'll be lucky if we don't get sick listening to him over the headphones"

Jake smiled. He just wanted this whole evening over with.

Lemar and Sands joined them about ten minutes later as they all sat and waited until they heard Stein mutter that he had arrived. They heard the car door slam and then the heavy rain in the background. A doorbell rang and then a man's voice,

"What the fuck are you doing here? I told you not to come while you are still sick"

"The doc says I'm not contagious anymore" Stein answered back.

"Fuck the doctor. You're not coming in. Stand there in the porch way. I'll go get the package. Have you got the cash?"

Silence and then the sound of rustling paper.

"No, I don't want your fuckin germs, throw the bag into the hallway. $4000 it better be all there"

"Yeah boss" a feeble voice came over the wire.

"Stay there, do not come in"

Indiscriminate mumbling could be heard as the voice got further and further away.

"Here, now get the fuck out of my sight."

The front door slammed and the listeners heard footsteps, a car door open and then slam again. An engine started, reverse beeping and then the roar as the car sped up. For a while nothing was said, then,

"Fuck I did it! Fuck I did it!"

A sigh of relief was heard throughout the radio room interrupted by a radio call telling Central that MS had been sighted leaving his destination.

"Thank Christ" Jake retorted and lifted his hands "touchdown"

Jake and the crew met Stein at a shopping center to pick up the cocaine and remove the wire tap. The cocaine was taken into evidence and the task of documenting all that had been said began. Each of the Agents wrote reports stating what each one had done throughout the evening.

Ted came into the Jake's office followed by Lemar, Sands and the two-agent surveillance team. Ted had brought with him his famous Scotch Whiskey and six glasses.

"The beginning of the end" he toasted and then "we did it"!

The Nassau County Warrant for Bob Branson's arrest was obtained by the DEA task force, processed and approved by the US Attorney on November 19th, 1987.

The following morning, at 8:30am, the quiet neighborhood of Flower Hill, Port Washington Long Island, was lit up with blue and red lights as agents arrived at Branson's house from DEA, FBI, INS together with Local and State Police.

Jake, wearing a Police bullet proof vest, knocked on the front door. Bob Branson opened it dressed in jeans, a flannel shirt and white sneakers.

"Robert Branson, I am arresting you for the Criminal Sale of a Controlled Substance, cocaine which is a Code 1 Felony Charge. Please put your hands around your back."

Bob Branson didn't move for a few moments as he tried to take in the scene in front of him. He was quite dumbfounded and totally caught off guard.

"Mr Branson, your hands" Jake repeated as he read Branson his Miranda Warning.

"What the fuck is going on" Branson angrily looked at Jake.

"Sir, everything will be explained to you, in full, at the Nassau Police Department" Jake applied the handcuffs and guided Branson to one of the numerous Police Cars at the scene.

At the same time, Branson's wife, Sherry came running out the front door, fresh from the shower, her wet hair halfway wrapped in a towel.

"Bob, Bob, what's going on?" she yelled as her husband was bowed down to get into an officers car. He immediately stood upright,

"Call Brian, have him meet me at Nassau County Police Department. Tell him what's going down"

"What's going down Bob?" she yelled.

"Just get Brian, now" he shouted as he was assisted into the Police car.

With the excitement over, all the agents returned to their cars, turned off their flashing lights and slowly left the neighborhood as they found it, peaceful and quiet.

By 2pm the same day, Bob Branson stood next to his attorney Brain Solowitz in front of the Judge in Nassau County District Court. Due to the relatively small amounts of cocaine, the AUSA Anthony Morgan had recommended that the case be dealt with at a local level rather than federally. Branson was charged with 2 Counts in the first degree of Sale of a Controlled Substance together with 2 Counts of Possession of a Controlled Substance.

Branson took the plea of not guilty and was released on his own recognizance. It was ordered that Robert Branson would appear before a grand jury on March 17, 1988. The same document ordered that Michael Stein be subpoenaed to testify at the proceedings in Nassau County Court, New York.

Jake then obtained warrants for Endario and D'Abrevio. He called them both on a recorded line and told them he had obtained their green cards and to meet him at Potter Park in Valley Stream. Agents from the FBI and INS were hidden and would move at the signal of Agent Taylor opening his car trunk. Both Endario and D'Abrevio arrived at Potter Park driving an old station wagon. Taylor opened his car window and beckoned the Italians to join him in his car. He presented each one with a green card, at the same time hitting the switch on his dash to open the trunk. Agents swarmed the car and arrested Endario and D'Abrevio. Each were transported to the Manhattan INS office, fingerprinted and photographed. They were searched before leaving the office, again in separate vehicles and transported to the US Courthouse Eastern District of New York in Brooklyn. On route, both blamed the other for getting involved in the scheme. Both were arraigned for Violation of the Federal Bribery Statue and committing an offense against the United States in violation of Title 18, United States Code 201(b) (1)(A).

Both were released on a $25,000 personal recognizance bond.

The Israelis for whom Jake he had obtained Alien Registration Cards, suffered the same fate.

It had been almost a month since Jake had heard from Stein. He knew that he was working with a DEA agent in order to build a case against Branson. Stein was aware that he would have to testify at Branson's hearing as he was instrumental in getting Branson arrested. The DEA were satisfied at the cooperation from Stein and an indictment of Branson on March 17, 1988, was anticipated.

On March 8th, 1988 Jake was about to leave his condo for the Garden City office when he received a disturbing phone call advising him that he needed to report to Nassau County Medical Center. He was advised that a car was in route and would collect him from his Condo within twenty minutes. The caller had no more information.

Jake grabbed his briefcase and his coat, and headed to the front of his building. By the time he got there, a black unmarked sedan pulled up in front of him, he recognized Ted Caturo sat in the back seat and Jake sat down in the seat next to him. The car pulled away from the building.

"Special Agent Taylor, your informant, Michael Stein was shot three times at his place of work. According to witnesses, Stein, parked his vehicle in the one of the bays and walked to the office door. An armed assailant, an unidentified black male, appeared from out of the office and opened fire with six rounds from a .38 caliber revolver. Stein was hit three times, one bullet caused a through and through injury to his left arm, the second remains lodged in his right side and another in his right hip. He was flown by police helicopter to Nassau Medical Center in critical condition and is currently in surgery. The gunman fled the scene dumping the firearm in a trash can in the front of the car wash and a ski cap and dark jacket was discarded as he ran. It can be assumed that the motive for this is directly related to Branson's upcoming trial with Stein being the prime witness"

"Jesus, Sir, is he going to make it?" Jake exclaimed

"It's too early to say. We will see what the doctors say when we get there. There is a guard posted outside of the operating suite, as well as his room."

"Stein anticipated this. He always told me that Branson threatened anyone that he thought was fooling around with him. He told Stein that he would set the "big guys" on him and that he wouldn't survive."

"If he survives this Jake, I want you to get him into the DEA Federal Witness Protection Program as soon as possible"

"With the greatest respect Sir, I doubt very much that he will enter into the program. All his family and friends are here on Long Island and in Queens. This is his identity"

They arrived at the hospital and immediately met with the Director outside Stein's room. The surgery was over and successful. He was in a stable but guarded condition. He had lost a lot of blood and was still asleep from the anesthetic.

"Can I speak to him Doc?" Jake enquired.

"Yes, as soon as we wakes up, but be gentle, don't talk too long, he needs rest to recover. If you can call a guy that has been shot three times "lucky," then lucky he is"

The doctor walked away as Jake quietly walked into Stein's hospital room. He was wearing an oxygen mask and had tubes coming from both arms. He was noticeably pale but very peaceful as he lay asleep. Jake sat down next to the bed his stomach queasy with both guilt and sadness. Stein had become an odd kind of friend over the past two years of working together.

Stein began to stir in the bed.

Jake beckoned to the nurse, who sat at a small table between Stein's room and the room next door.

"Mr. Stein, do you know where you are?"

Without waiting for an answer, she continued,

"You are at Nassau County Medical Center where you just underwent surgery. How are you feeling?"

Stein turned his head slowly to look at her,

"Like someone shot me"

He noticed Jake as he turned his head,

"What did I tell you? I knew he'd come. The worst part was the waiting. Motherfucker"

"Mike, the DEA and Eastern District of New York have offered you a place in the Federal Witness Protection Program which I seriously think you should consider"

"You know me better than that Jake. I ain't going nowhere. I'll testify then I'll disappear where I want to, with who I want to"

"They've already postponed the hearing to June 9th so you can recover" Jake acknowledged

"Shit, no. Don't let them do that. I need to get this behind me and move on man"

"Too late Mike, they already rescheduled. You will have full protection while you are here in the hospital and when you get home, if you change your mind, we can continue to protect you and settle you and your wife in another part of the Country"

"Diana left weeks ago. She's staying with her sister in Queens. She won't be back. If I disappear, they will go after my brother and my mother. Ain't worth it man"

Jake understood and nodded his head,

"What can I get you Mike?"

"A beer and my mother's meatballs. No, I'm good man, can't eat yet. I gotta get some sleep. I feel terrible"

The nurse appeared once again out of nowhere.

"Officer" she looked directly at Jake

"Special Agent actually Ma'am. I'm with the F.B.I." Jake flipped open his credentials.

"Well, whoever you are, I need you to leave and let Mr. Stein get some sleep"

"Yes Ma'am" Jake stood up, winked at Mike and left the room. "I'll be back tomorrow Mike. Don't get into any trouble, you hear"

"Yea right", Stein groaned as he tried to change position.

Ted Caturo and Jake returned to the Garden City Office in the same car. Jake enlightened his supervisor that Stein would not take the offer of the Witness Protection program as he had suggested earlier.

"Do we have anything on the shooter yet Sir?"

"We do have a lead on a Pete Green who does have ties to Branson. Green is also wanted in Ohio for charges relating to the sale of cocaine and he is scheduled to appear in Georgia on ATF gun charges. We have an APB out but he's gone underground".

"What can I do Sir?" Jake took out a pad from his brief case to take notes.

"Jake, we have received a call from District Director Fava. You are temporarily off this case and you are to report to your office tomorrow morning at the Federal Building in Manhattan and report to Agent Dave Valerio"

This news hit Jake like a brick. What was going on now? He had proved his innocence from the false accusations of working as a lifeguard while on the clock with the FBI. He had been totally exonerated and the United States Attorney's office had declined to prosecute. Feeling sick to his stomach, he stood up and offered his hand to his supervisor Ted Caturo.

Ted shook his hand, promised Jake he would keep him appraised on the condition of Stein and the investigation on the shooter. Jake would also have to return for the trial of Robert Branson on June 9th.

Chapter Seven

Jake returned to his former office in Manhattan. He hadn't slept all night. He wore a black suit indicative of his mood. As he walked the length of the office, agents lifted their heads. Some looked down immediately, others nodded but no one spoke. Jake found his cubicle, put his brief case down and sat at his desk. Almost immediately, Agent Valerio entered his cubicle and advised that Jake needed to attend a briefing immediately in the conference room.

Jake picked up his briefcase and followed Valerio into the conference room. Already seated at the large table was a young lady in front of a typewriter. As Valerio began to speak, the young lady began to type.

"Agent Taylor, I am giving you today, a form G-792 which you have a week to complete. You are currently the subject of an administrative investigation, regarding specific dates whereby you have stated that you were working for the United States Federal Government, yet our investigation has found you working, at the exact same times, for the Long Beach Lifeguard Association. You are to submit the completed form to myself in seven days and then you are ordered to appear at an administration hearing on March 21st, 1988. Do you understand Agent Taylor"?

"Actually, no I do not understand Agent Valerio. From the brief look at the dates you have requested, they are virtually the same dates which were the subject of the US Attorney's office declination to prosecute"

"Agent Taylor, I will not discuss this matter until your hearing on March 21st, 1988" Valerio seemed undaunted.

"Fair enough, I will complete your form and I will attend the hearing with counsel" Jake stood up and turned to walk away.

"Before you leave Agent Taylor, I need to you to surrender your service revolver"

"On what grounds?" Jake retorted.

"You, are under investigation Agent Taylor. That's all the grounds I need".

Jake reached under his jacket and produced the revolver. He unloaded the weapon rendering it safe, placed on the table and turned to the young lady typing.

"Make sure that my actions regarding my weapon are documented Ma'am."

"Yes Sir" she replied as she continued to type.

Jake walked out of the conference room, picked up his coat from his cubicle and walked out of 26 Federal Plaza. Furious, was an understatement when it came to Jake's mood. He walked across Manhattan trying to maintain his demeanor. Although a cool early spring day, Jake was sweating by the time he reached the office of Attorney Roger Aparrone.

"Is he in?" Jake inquired of the young paralegal assigned to Roger.

"Yes he is, but he's in a meeting"

"I'll wait" Jake sat down, took off his suit jacket, loosened his tie and unbuttoned the top button of his shirt.

"Can I get you some water"? the paralegal looked concerned "you look very hot".

"Water would be good, thanks".

Roger looked incredulous as Jake recounted his meeting with Valerio in the conference room.

"I don't get it. We have already disproven this with the agencies own records. How can he ignore those facts? This has turned into a vendetta"

"Roger, I looked at the dates he is requesting my activities, all but one we have proven that I completed service work"

"Then we will fill out his dates, submit the same evidence and figure out what you were doing in the new date. I will represent you at your hearing on March 21st and we will finally show Valerio for what he is"

"One other thing Roger, they have revoked my rights to carry a weapon. I was ordered to surrender my service weapon before I left the office."

"Jesus Jake, he really does hate you. Go home, have a drink. We'll talk soon"

It didn't take long to compile the paperwork for the meeting on March 21st as it was all duplicated from

Roger's meeting with the US Attorney where it had been decided not to prosecute Jake. There was just one date that Jake could not determine what he was doing. The date in question was almost six years prior and nothing was documented in Jake's diary. It seemed the payroll from Long Beach had been lost. Jake was not going to allow himself to be caught in a lie, so he simply told Roger that he could not recollect what he had done on that date six years ago.

Jake was in no mood to entertain his mother on March 20th, 1988. Her birthday fell on March 21st, but due to the hearing he had decided to take her out the night before. He had wanted to cook for her at her condo, but his mother was having none of that.

"I've been on this earth for 67 years and raised four children. I deserve a night out with my son" she told him very specifically on the telephone.

"Ok Mom but we are not going to Victor's again"

Afraid of being tailed, he did not want to give Valerio anything which he could use against him. Victor would just love being interviewed about a dirty Federal Agent.

They decided on a small restaurant in Rockfield Centre, Dario's. Dario and his son were friends of Jake and would leave them in peace, plus if interviewed, Jake knew they had his back.

"You're awfully quiet tonight Jake. It's my birthday tomorrow, not my funeral. I saw your sister Kate today. I told her that my warm winter coat, is not keeping me warm anymore. She gave me $100 to buy a new one. I also talked to Pam, she's doing the same. They appreciate their dear old mother and what she's been through"

Jake opened his wallet. This was the same line his mother used on him every time she needed money. If his sister gave $100, he had to give $200 because he was not married and had no children.

He placed $200 cash the table in front of his mother.

"Awww really Jake. What a nice surprise. I'll have to talk to your other sister Eunice. Perhaps you could take me into Manhattan tomorrow and we can go shopping?"

"I can't Mom; I have some important meetings tomorrow"

"What, more important than your Mother? Your old mother who worked all her life and struggled to take care of you and your sisters"

"Just not tomorrow Mom, please, let it go"

An awkward silence came between them until Dario burst out of the kitchen with a lighted candle in the top of a birthday cake. With the waiters and waitresses in tow, they all sang happy birthday as Jake's mother, quite obviously loving the attention, as others turned from their tables to see who was celebrating.

March 21st was a brutally cold day. It seemed the weather could not decide what season it should be in. The hearing was scheduled at 3pm at the Federal Building. Jake was to meet Roger at 2:30pm in the lobby.

To try and take his mind off what lay ahead, Jake decided to drive to the Garden City office to how inquiries were going related to Mike Stein shooting. Over the radio, he heard the office ask him to call the main switch board. He decided to ignore the call and continued on to Garden City. The second call over the radio sounded a little more urgent requesting that Special Agent Taylor call into the office immediately.

Jake pulled over and called the office. The receptionist answered and told him that his mother had been mugged in Manhattan and was at the Manhattan South Police Precinct.

Jake flipped his emergency red lights on and sped back into Manhattan and found his mother talking to a female officer.

"Here he is, I told you he would come. This is my son, the one with the FBI. This is Officer Denton, Jake. She's single"

"What happened Mom" as he threw a quick smile at Officer Denton who was grinning at him.

"Well no one wanted to take me to Manhattan to buy a coat so I came on the train. Some man ran straight at me and pulled my purse off my shoulder. He was too fast or I would have punched him"

Jake rolled his eyes;

"How much cash did you have on you Mom?"

"Well, your sister Eunice gave me $100, Kate gave me $100 and so did Pam. You gave me $200" she turned and smiled at Officer Denton, "he earns more working for the FBI"

"Mom, you had $500 cash in your purse?"

"I told you I needed a new coat"

Jake sat down shaking his head. Officer Denton had already taken his mother's statement so after a few more signatures; Jake thanked Officer Denton and walked out into the cold street.

"I'll take you home Mom"

He looked down at this little old lady with white curly hair

 "But I have my government car so I will have to put handcuffs on you and you will have to act like a prisoner. It's a 45-day suspension for the misuse of a government vehicle".

Immediately, Jake's mother put her hands together and offered them to Jake.

"I was kidding Mom, get in". He opened the front passenger and petite little body slid into the passenger seat.

Smiling, he got in next to her, telling her that he'd hoped that she had learned her lesson.

Once his mom was back home safely and already on the phone to his sister Kate, Jake headed back to Manhattan.

He barely made the 2:30pm meeting time in the lobby. He arrived to find Roger going through the metal detectors.

"I thought you had given up and turned yourself in"

"No, I was just rescuing an old lady who had been mugged in Manhattan.

Puzzled Roger looked at Jake, but he was already two paces ahead of Roger heading towards the elevators.

For the next two hours, Jake and Roger proceeded to go through the dates that Valerio had stated Jake had "double dipped" from both the US Government and

Long Beach. Predictably, Valerio could not provide a single affidavit or memorandum of contact for any of the dates. The last date in question, Jake simply said that he could remember what he was doing then six years ago. Valerio closed the meeting and advised both Jake and Roger that they would be apprised of the decision within five working days.

Roger was guardedly optimistic about the proceedings and shared this with Jake. Jake was, as expected, convinced that these injustices would continue.

On the fourth day after the hearing, Jake received notice that he had to appear the following day at the office of the District Director Fava at the Federal Building.

Although confident in the fact that he had proven his innocence, Jake and his attorney Roger were somewhat apprehensive as they walked into Director Fava's office. Of course, Agent Valerio was present.

Before they had even got comfortably seated, Valerio stood up and welcomed Jake and Roger to the meeting. Jake rolled his eyes.

Valerio, on his soap box, waffled on and on about the integrity of the Justice Department and the need for transparency …. He turned and looked at Jake,

"Agent Taylor. Is it true that in order to exonerate you from the charges presented on March 21st, you presented documentation from your personal diaries?"

Without even waiting a reply, he went on,

"Is that not so, Agent Taylor?"

"Yes sir, together with internal documentation to prove their authenticity" Jake replied.

"Personal diaries written about government business" he gloated.

He turned to Roger and stated,

"We will be recommending termination for your client due to the unlawful disclosure of government records, i.e., your diaries" Valerio smiled and turned his stare to look at Jake.

"How did I unlawfully disclose these records when I only disclosed them to you." Jake demanded.

"We both know this is untrue Agent Taylor. You disclosed these records to Assistant US Attorney Sally Johnson at the time the Government was about to charge you, and you continue to disclose them to a civilian even now. I believe Attorney Aparrone has also seen these records, hence unlawful disclosure"

"I must strongly object to this, Agent Valerio. The only way Agent Taylor could prove his innocence was through his personal diaries" Roger argued.

"Those diaries contain sensitive classified government records which have been unlawfully disclosed. This demands immediate termination Attorney Aparrone"

"District Director Fava, I cannot believe what I am hearing. This is a sham" Roger's voice now increasing decibels with every word.

"Attorney Aparrone, your client will have one week to prove these charges are not true. Should he be unable to do so, he will terminated forthwith. Good day gentlemen" Fava stood up behind his desk and beckoned to Jake and Roger to leave the room.

Silently, Jake and Roger left the building. They both seemed shell shocked by the charges leveled at Jake. They returned to Roger's office.

"Are you ok?" Roger broke the silence.

"I don't know" Jake whispered. "I need to go home and figure this out"

"I will prepare a strong rebuttal. I will be in touch tomorrow Jake".

Jake emotionless, found his car and began the drive home through the Manhattan traffic. His head was throbbing and without realizing he began to rub his chest. He grabbed a couple of aspirins from the center console. The radio came alive with a message that Agent Taylor needed to return to the Federal Building and surrender his government car. Jake pulled over and got out of the car. He paced up and down the embankment still rubbing his chest. He felt sick, defeated, tired and exploited. The pain in his chest intensified and began to affect his left arm. As if brought back to his senses, he realized something was very wrong.

"No, Valerio, you are not about to kill me" he muttered out loud. He got back into the car, hit his lights and sirens and drove to the ER at St Francis Medical Center. He was seen immediately by Dr James Klein. The barrage of tests was overwhelming to Jake. He asked one of the candy striper girls to ring his friend and fellow Special Agent Rick.

Rick got there just as they were rolling Jake to the Cath lab for a cardiac catheterization.

"Shit man, what the hell happened? The radio is going wild. The office is trying to get hold of you"

"They haven't killed me yet Rick. Can you call the office and tell them what's going on?"

"Are you sure Jake?"

"If you don't, I expect they will put out a warrant for my arrest."

"Good luck in there Man. I'll be out here waiting for you to be done"

Rick called the office and informed them of what had happened. The first question they had for Rick

"Is the government car safe?"

"Are you fucking kidding me? Is the car safe? Fuck the car. Your officer is fighting for his life"

"I would be careful to what you say next, Special Agent. Please secure the car and return it to the office immediately".

"If you want the car, you come and get it yourselves. I'm busy and off duty" Rick slammed down the receiver and returned to the cath lab waiting area.

Feeling extremely vulnerable and very naked, Jake, lay flat on his back, tried to make polite conversation with the nurse who was shaving his groin area prior to the procedure. The room was cold and full of white machines. As Jake looked around, he realized everything was white and sterile looking. There was a strong odor of rubbing alcohol and disinfectant. As he gazed up at the large procedure light, a booming voice shocked him.

"Agent Terry. I'm Doc Metz. Can I ask you a favor"?

"Doc, you have me at a disadvantage here. I'll do whatever you need" Jake replied

"Could you get me an F.B.I. baseball cap?" the Doc's booming voice echoing around the large room.

"Hell Doc, I'll get you a shirt and jacket too if you get me through this" Jake quipped back.

The following day, after Jake's discharge with a diagnosis of Mitral Valve Prolapse, Rick drove Jake home to his condo.

"Can I get anything for you pal? I can run down to the deli"

"I'm good; I just want to get some rest. I'll call Janice later, she'll help me. Thanks for getting me home; you're a good friend Rick"

Jake made a call into his attorney's office and was put right through to Roger. He explained what had happened at the hospital. Roger was not surprised. He told Jake that he was writing a strong rebuttal. He had contacted the Long Beach Chief lifeguard, Steve Kyot. Steve had collected the affidavits from the lifeguards who had been interviewed by Valerio. Roger told Jake that he was shocked at the lifeguard's contradictions. He believed that, this in itself, questioned Valerio's summary recitation of what he had claimed the lifeguards had stated. He also questioned the fairness of the interviews and statements which the lifeguards had given, later surmising that Valerio had tried to put words into their mouths. He also reported speaking to other friends and colleagues of Jake who had attested to his integrity and outstanding character. He asked Jake to put together a file with letters of recognition as well as annual appraisals from his time with the Justice Department.

Armed with these numerous statements and affidavits, Roger requested a meeting with District Director Fava. This was denied and he was told to submit the evidence to Fava's office. Fortunately Jake was still off work under a doctor's note from his procedure at the hospital so he was unable to go to Fava's office. He simply put them in the mail.

Within a week, Jake received a letter from the District Director. The letter stated that most of the charges per Valerio were sustained, however, rather than impose termination, Jake would be put on unpaid suspension for forty-five days. As furious as Jake was, he also realized that this would also affect the trial for Bob Branson. The trial had already been moved back due to Stein's shooting, it would now have to be moved back once more due to Jake's suspension.

After he had filled Roger in with the details of the suspension, Jake told him that he would be filing a grievance immediately. His next call was to Mike Stein, now back home convalescing after the shooting. Careful not to divulge the suspension, Jake advised him that he had heard that a continuance had been requested for the trial. Surprisingly Stein sounded comfortable with the move. After some prodding, Jake realized that Stein feared that his life was in danger on the day of the trial. Jake reassured him that he would be protected, but for him to recover in the meantime.

Through the correct channels, Jake filed a grievance with the Justice Department. He provided all the documentation which Roger had filed with the District Director, together with a sworn affidavit that the charges against him were false.

Within a week, Jake received a notice of Arbitration hearing at the beginning of June, 1988. As this was an internal arbitration, Roger would not be allowed to attend. During the wait for the hearing Jake experienced so many emotions. He was furious at how Valerio had manipulated the system twice in an obvious vendetta, yet he was saddened and hurt on how some of his colleagues had turned their backs on him, even spoken out against him with the promise of promotion. He tried to take his mind off things by socializing with other friends but somehow, he always ended up regretting going in the first place.

After going over the files time and time again to be absolutely ready, he received a call on the eve of the hearing from the arbitrator in his case, Attorney Jack Johnson. Attorney Johnson advised him that the hearing, due to total lack of merit and the obvious embarrassment which it would incur to the FBI, the Justice Department, by stipulation, rescinded Jake's suspension. They had also agreed to remove and expunge from Jake's file, all references to the suspension and the allegations and reports on which the suspension was based. They agreed to reimburse Jake in accordance to the provisions of the Back Pay Act with interest and restoration of any applicable leave. Added to this they would pay Jake $12,500 to resolve the issues of Attorney fees and costs.

Jake couldn't call Roger quick enough. The FBI's total capitulation on every issue spoke volumes about the lack of merit of the case and the shoddy, unfair and unprofessional manner in which Agent Valerio had conducted his investigation. In addition to not supporting his allegations with a single memorandum of contact or affidavit, in his blindness to get Jake, Valerio disclosed and used, in the administrative process, materials and information obtained by the grand jury thus violating the FBI's own guidelines as well as the law governing grand jury secrecy.

Jake returned to his office the following Monday. Even though he had been completely exonerated from all the charges, no one congratulated him, no one jumped up to shake his hand. In fact, not a sound could be heard as Jake walked through the office with a large paper under his arm. Once in his cubicle, Jake unfolded the large paper revealing a blown-up copy of the $12,500 check issued by the FBI to pay Jake's attorney fees. Above the check was a copy of a letter written and printed in the Professional Journal of the Federal Law Enforcement Officers Association:

Dear Editor

On October 16th, 1984, I was sworn into the US Customs as a Special Agent, along with 24 other men and women. I never acquired that position because during a routine background check, which evolved into months of inquiries and resulted in innuendoes and falsehoods, a conflict was found to exist between my employment as a Special Agent and my second employment as a lifeguard with the City of Long Beach, NY.

This lasted from October 1985 to September 1989. In September 1989, my 45-day suspension was rescinded, reimbursement made of my back pay with interest, my leave restored and compensation awarded for legal fees, I received a check for $12,500. I endured a David and Goliath struggle with the Justice Department to prove my innocence and to regain my reputation.

In the process, I encountered a bureaucracy, that not only allowed but encouraged, unfounded charges to mushroom. My name was smeared. My neighbors and friends became alarmed at the seemingly endless questions they were asked. Individuals with whom I had close contact, avoided me. For the first time, I received a less than favorable rating; an award was temporarily "lost"; another award was denied and I was systematically passed over for promotions.

Some individuals, including past and present Management, looked on at these obvious injustices because they did not have the courage or integrity to chance political disfavor. Their egos and ambitions blocked my attempts to vindicate myself.

At the same time, other individuals and colleagues with whom I have had contact stood strong and supported me. To those fellow workers who believed in me and never quit on me, I can only say for myself and my family, "Thank you."

Although I sincerely hope no colleague ever endures even a part of what I have endured during the last five years, I would like everyone to know that it is possible to triumph over the Goliaths in Government with the five smooth stones of perseverance.

I am looking forward to writing the final chapter on this experience....no matter how long it takes.

Sincerely,

Jake Taylor, Special Agent
US Justice Department,
New York, NY

He attached the paper to the front of the cubicle for all to see, sat down at his desk and began to catch up on the Branson case. He contacted Garden City and advised what had happened with his suspension. Ted Caturo told Jake that he was still under the special detail to the INS but couldn't return to the office until he was armed again. Jake immediately put in a request to be issued a fire arm together with a request for the return of his government car. His Glock gun was reissued the same day, however every time he followed up about the car, he got the runaround. Eventually, he discovered that Valerio had denied the request due to "Agent Jake Taylor's recent heart attack." In fact, Valerio had not just denied the return of Jake's government car, he had advised that Jake could not even ride in a government car.

Jake immediately sent an inter-office memo stating he had not had a heart attack and that in fact, he had recently won five gold medals at the New York Police Summer Olympics. He also pointed out that his follow up stress test had stated he could resume full duties. Of course, this was not good enough for Valerio, who insisted upon another stress test. Infuriated, Jake sent a memo to the District Director Fava stating that Valerio was continuing his vendetta against him, explaining that other Agents, who really had suffered a heart attack and worse, were allowed to drive government vehicles. Expecting the request to be over turned, Jake was mortified to find out that Director Fava was now questioning his psychological status, stating that Jake believed that everyone was out to get him. Not only did he now have endure another stress test, now he had been referred to a psychiatrist for testing.

Jake was totally overwhelmed. He felt betrayed by the service which he had devoted himself to for the past ten years and abandoned by his coworkers who he had enjoyed such good relationships with in the past. The only one who stood by him was Rick. Rick told him that his friends in the service had been threatened with serious ramifications if they were supportive of Jake and any criticism of Valerio would jeopardize their careers. Valerio had become known as the "hit man" for the service, out to get Jake. Seeing the results of what he was doing with Jake, was enough to keep everyone else quiet. Rick's advice was to lay low, see the psychiatrist, have the stress test then put in for a transfer to another agency.

The summer of 1988 was just around the corner. At least Jake could look forward to his weekends on the beach as a lifeguard. The beach opened Memorial Day and lasted through Labor Day. For the past sixteen years, Jake would work every day he was not working for the government, on the beach. This year, however, was the first time he had to complete a form requesting authorization to work for outside employment. Most of the agents had summer positions, many working for their family businesses, so this new authorization was an inconvenience for everyone.

Jake completed his stress test with flying colors and finally got his government car back. The same day he received a letter from Director Fava denying Jake's formal request to work as a lifeguard during the summer months. The letter stated, once again that it was "demeaning and unprofessional for a Special Agent to work as a lifeguard". Jake was furious and immediately appealed the decision sending a picture of President Reagan working as a lifeguard in his youth. The Chief Lifeguard from Long Beach, Steve Kyot also wrote on Jake's behalf…denied denied denied!

Dr. Ian McDonald a workplace psychiatrist, at first had a hard time believing Jake until he produced supporting documentation which proved and substantiated everything Jake had said. Dr. McDonald told Jake that in his many years of practicing he had never seen such blatant misuse of power and such brutal attacks on an employee. He told Jake that he was not angry enough! Most patients of Dr McDonald tried to prove themselves unfit for work, Jake was just the opposite, he just wanted to go back. He told Jake that if he won the Medal of Honor, he would not receive it if Fava and Valerio were in charge. Finally, Jake could verbalize his emotional pain and his feelings of abandonment without fear it would be used against him. Dr. McDonald reasoned with Jake that if the FBI really believed the charges Valerio had set forth in March 1986, they would have never allowed Jake to initiate or continue the Adonis investigation.

The investigation into Jake's history had now expanded into a joint investigation with the FBI, and later on, with the DEA. Also the INS, had permitted and indeed encouraged, Jake to risk his life daily as an undercover Agent in the investigation. Due to the dubious nature of the charges going back to 1985 and the shaky documentary foundations on which they were based, the service had deemed Jake unreliable. Now during the Adonis investigation, with the cooperation from the INS, FBI and DEA, all recognized the true and continued reliability, trustworthiness and professional excellence of Jake.

Encouraged with the advice offered by Dr. McDonald, Jake contacted the Assistant Director of the FBI in Washington, DC. He was granted a face-to-face meeting to discuss the investigation and charges levied by Valerio. Attorney Roger Aparrone would be permitted to join Jake in the meeting.

Jake hated flying but needed to get Roger back to New York after the meeting. He also had to fund the trip himself so to cut back on his mounting attorney fees. In his fear of flying, Jake had always believed that a prop plane was the safest way to fly. He rationalized this by thinking that if the engines failed, the plane would glide until it landed. He called Roger's secretary to tell her that he had found a prop plane to take them to Washington. Within minutes of him hanging up the phone, Roger called, and in no uncertain terms, informed Jake that he was not flying on a prop plane. Within 60 seconds, Roger disputed and then destroyed Jake's entire rationalization of a safe prop plane.

Two days later, Jake and Roger took the Eastern Shuttle Express to Washington DC. Jake rented a car at the airport and drove into the city. They made a brief stop at a McDonalds to grab a bite to eat and were shocked to find an armed guard at the door. The guard told them that crime in the DC was out of control and that no one was safe in the city after dark.

Assistant Director Joseph Ferendenus felt that he had done his homework on Jake but was shocked and incredulous as Jake explained in detail, over the next hour, the timeline of events over the past years. Although in total agreement with Jake and Roger with regard to the blatant injustice, he advised that, due to the upcoming Presidential election and subsequent administration change, Jake would have to wait before any significant steps could be taken to stop Valerio. He advised Jake that once the new administration were seated, he would recommend him for a promotion to OCDETF (Organized Crime and Drug Enforcement Task Force) in New York putting Jake out of Valerio's reach for the rest of his career. For the first time in years, Jake felt validated.

The old feelings of excitement and pride within Jake, were evident to Roger as the two of them traveled back to New York on the last shuttle out of DC. Although Jake had been reluctant to seek the help of a psychiatrist, Dr. McDonald had given him the strength and resilience to continue the fight. Jake returned to work with a healthy psychological diagnosis and a clean bill of health. Dr McDonald had recommended he return to work immediately and documented this to Director Fava.

Chapter Eight

Upon Jake's return to the Federal Building in Manhattan, his detail to the Garden City INS was renewed. Now armed and with a government vehicle, Jake returned to Garden City and received a rousing round of applause as he walked through the office for the first time in a month.

News on the shooter in the attempted murder of Michael Stein was the first item of business for Jake. Peter Green had been named as the chief suspect in the case. All the evidence led to Bob Branson hiring Green to shoot Shapiro. Unfortunately, charges could not be fought against Green as he had subsequently been arrested in Ohio in drug charges and sentenced for ten years. On top of this, he was being transferred to Georgia to face trial on ATF gun charges which would add another ten years to his sentence to run concurrently. Peter Green was off the streets for some time which gave Jake some solace.

Bill Branson's court date had been rescheduled again due to Jake's suspension, however, the court date for Lorenzo Endario and Jusieppi D'Abrevio had been scheduled for September 27, 1988. This court date also included thirteen other aliens which Jake had worked with in conjunction with Stein. In the end, the thirteen avoided prosecution and were subsequently deported to their Countries of Origin. Endario and D'Abrevio were sentenced to three years' incarceration with two years nine months suspended. Upon serving the sentence, they were also deported.

Ready now to move forward with the Branson court case, Jake contacted Mike Stein to review the case and to prep him for the hearing at the Nassau County District Court.

Stein was pleased to see Jake as they met at a local diner. Jake told him about Pete Green and explained why they could not press charges until he was transferred to Georgia. Although the evidence pointed to Bill Branson as the instigator, he also could not be charged due to Green's situation. Stein although relieved, told Jake that it was just a matter of time until there was another attempt on his life. He'd bought a large German Shepherd dog, Thor, with the hope that Thor would protect him. His wife had filed for divorce and was living with his children at her mother's. Jake felt bad for Mike, but there was no turning back. Jake continued to talk about the case and explained that he would go to trial, once Branson had been convicted. He did not expect that Stein would do serious time as he had spoken to the prosecutor and explained that he had cooperated fully in cases related to INS fraud and bribery together with drug trafficking. Unfortunately, Jake was not going to be in court for the Branson case so to keep his cover as a corrupt Federal Agent.

The Nassau County District Court was standing room only as Mike Stein took the witness stand in the case against Bob Branson. Stein had told to Jake that all the "Big Boys" would be there. Obviously to put pressure on Stein, Branson had arranged as many thugs on his payroll to come to his hearing. Stein was terrified. Stein's lawyer, Benjamin Pello tried to calm him by instructing him to look straight at him as he testified and to tell the truth.

"Remember you are not just here to get a conviction for Branson, you are also here to save your own skin. Don't let them get to you"

"They put a dead rat on my front porch Ben. I had to pry it out of Thor's mouth in case it was poisoned" Mike whispered back.

Before questioning Stein, the Judge warned that any outbursts in the court room would not be tolerated and that it would result in immediate expulsion from the room.

Stein answered each question truthfully and was asked to speak up numerous times. Each time he did, there was a crescendo of coughing and people clearing their voices in the gallery. The judge once again, sternly warned against any outbursts and asked the bailiffs to remove anyone who even attempted to cough.

By the time Stein sat back down next to Ben he was actually shaking with fear and perspiring profusely.

"It's over" Ben reassured him.

Branson convicted for the Sale of a Controlled Substance, a Class B felony, was taken away in handcuffs to serve one and a half to four and a half years. As he was lead out of court, he turned looked at Stein, threw his head back and laughed.

Stein's court date was scheduled the following month, however, with the case almost closed, Jake's detail with the INS was terminated. He returned to the Federal Building in Manhattan to resume his position in the FBI. He would return for the Stein court date to testify in behalf of the government.

Within a week of his return to Manhattan he received copies of letters written by the US Attorney,

Department of the Treasury, Nassau County District Attorney, US Customs and the US Department of Justice complimenting Jake on his hard work, expertise and professionalism. Each letter focused on Jake's ability to work outside of his normal scope and enhance the investigative efforts of three Federal Agencies and a local enforcement agency as well as a willingness to give up an enormous amount of personal time to insure his work was successful. Through a single bribe overture, good investigative work and going the "extra step" he was able to develop cases involving violations of narcotic laws, conspiracy, attempted extortion and Immigration violations which had resulted in the arrests of fifteen individuals. In addition to this, one of the individuals arrested was the victim of an attempted murder due to him introducing Jake to a narcotics dealer.

During Jake's latter time at the Garden City INS detail, District Director Fava of the FBI retired. Director Fava and Special Agent Valerio had worked together to terminate Jake on false accusations. Jake had proven the accusations to be false through official FBI documentation, embarrassing both of them. With Fava being out of the picture, Jake felt that he could move on from this and continue moving upward with his career. Bob Slaughterly had been promoted to District Director. Quickly, Slaughterly with his new ideas, deleted a number of key positions within the agency and created new opportunities for those who qualified for promotion.

Armed with his recent accolades from Codename Adonis, multiple other endorsements and fourteen years of exemplary yearly appraisals, Jake applied for the position of Supervisory Criminal Investigator. He met all of the qualifications, in fact he was the best qualified for the job and the most senior of all the applicants. Confident, although guardedly so, he was horrified to find that the position had been given to a junior agent, whom Jake had mentored and trained into the system. Disgusted, he knew that Valerio had something to do with this. He immediately filed a complaint with the EEO (Equal Employment Opportunity) commission. The week before the Commission was about to hear his complaint, Jake received an anonymous call from an unknown female. She advised him that she had seen, on a memo to Slaughterly, the words "trouble maker" next to Jake's name. Jake asked the female caller if she could get him a copy of the memo. She advised him that she already had it and would send it to his home address.

Although angry, Jake felt once again, he would be able to prove his case to the commission. Once again he felt alone, betrayed and exploited by the system.

That night as he drove home from Manhattan to Long Beach he had the uncanny feeling that he was being followed. He changed his normal route home and added various turns and detours. Still a little unnerved, he was really caught off guard when he saw Bob Branson, sat in a flashy Mercedes close to his condo building. He purposely drove past his building, parked in a municipal parking lot and walked home, entering the building through a back door. As he opened the door to his condo, his landline was ringing. He picked it up, without speaking and heard a click and then the dial tone at the other end. During the evening there were three more hang ups. Jake made a few calls and discovered that Branson had been released from incarceration the day before, he had only served thirty days. Jake immediately called Mike Stein with no success. He left a voice message advising that Mike call him as soon as possible.

Jake then called his former supervisor from the Garden City INS detail, Ted Caturo.

"You haven't heard Jake?" Ted asked

"Heard what?"

"Shit, my office called Director Slaughterly over an hour ago. They were supposed to call you. Stein was fatally shot multiple times this evening from unknown assailants. He must have crawled to his garage door and opened it setting off a silent alarm. We think that his German shepherd must have been in the garage. When the door was opened by Stein, the dog got out and chased one of the assailants. A neighbor found the dog dead from numerous bullet wounds near her back fence."

Jake sat down dumbfounded.

"I'm sorry Jake, I know you worked closely with the guy for a long time" Ted spoke sympathetically.

"His family?" Jake quietly enquired

"No one else home" Ted replied.

Jake recounted what he had transpired that evening with him.

"I'd get out of there man. They know who you are and where you are. I wouldn't take the chance"

Jake hung up, threw a few things into a bag and left the building through the back exit. Constantly surveilling his surroundings, he got to his car and drove back to his office in Manhattan. On the way, he checked in with his sisters and mother before sitting at his desk and writing up a full report.

Two days later and after two uncomfortable nights at the Holiday Inn, Jake received a fax from the Threat Investigation Office with an analysis of his threat potential.

The threat potential against Special Agent Taylor arose out of a lengthy case where and he posed as a corrupt Immigration Special Agent. This case, because of its bribery nexus, was handled by the FBI and the Office of Professional Responsibility. What follows is a history of that case and analysis of the threat potential it may pose to Special Agent Taylor.

General Background of the Case
The case began on January 31, 1986 when Michael Stein proprietor of the East Side Car Wash in Valley Stream, NY spoke with Agent Taylor, whom he knew from a 1981 area control operation about buying green cards for five individuals for the sum of $10,000

Agent Taylor appropriately reported this matter to the FBI Office of Professional responsibility who in turn reported it to the INS. The FBI, after consulting with the US Attorney's office, Eastern District of New York, took control of the investigation on February 7, 1986 and notified OPM that it would handle a request for consensual monitoring, manpower needs, and control of the undercover activities of Special Agent Taylor. The New York Office of Professional Responsibility subsequently provided back up support and facilitated the acquisition of "legitimate" I – 551 impression stamps and ultimately to green cards.

Initially, five employment authorization impression stamps were placed in five passports for the sum of $5000. These stamped impressions were obtained by the Office of Professional Responsibility, and this portion of the investigation was used to establish the credibility of Special Agent Taylor. In response to the requests from Stein for actual green cards, for which Taylor would be paid $5000 per card, it was decided to provide two legitimate green cards.

On March 21, 1986, Taylor was given an additional deposit of $2000 per card on the agreed-upon figure of $5000 by Stein on behalf of Lorenzo Endario, and Jusieppi D'Abrevio. Subsequent payments were made and the cards were ultimately delivered.

During the course of the bribery investigation, Special Agent Taylor was the subject of overtures by Stein , who wanted to know if Taylor was interested in dealing cocaine. Stein indicated that he had a supplier *by the name of Robert Branson who owned Six Towns Car Wash in Florence, NY. Branson. Branson, according to Stein , purchased cocaine by the kilo and subsequently distributed it. Based on this information the Drug Enforcement Administration (DEA) was notified and a decision was made to conduct a formal investigation based upon the intelligence provided by Special Agent Taylor.*

On September 16, 1986, Taylor spoke to Stein at his car wash and was given and additional $1000 payment on the green card previously mentioned. He was also given a small sample vial of cocaine. On December 5, 1986 at a meeting in Lister Park in Rockville center, New York, Taylor informed Stein that the sample he had been given was satisfactory. Stein told him that larger quantities could be obtained and that he would have as much cocaine as he wanted. Subsequently in December 1986 Taylor introduced DEA Special Agent Tania Rowen to Stein at his place of business, and 1 ounce of cocaine was purchased for $2000. On December 30 1986 Special Agent Taylor was called at his home by Stein, who said he was at Robert Branson's house and that he could have additional cocaine. Taylor told Stein to call back and did not receive a call back.

In February 1987 Stein called Taylor to inform him that Branson would supply a quarter pound of cocaine *for $7500. Taylor appropriately notified DEA. Subsequently in March 1987 Agent Taylor paid Stein $4000 for 2 ounces of cocaine, which was delivered in March 1987.*

Stein was subsequently arrested and as part of a plea agreement was allowed to plead guilty to one count of conspiracy to bribe a federal agent in return for his cooperation against Robert Branson, who was subsequently arrested in 1987. A decision was made by DEA to transfer Branson's case to Nassau County for trial on state charges, since the penalties on the state charges in this particular case were more severe than Federal charges.

Days later, Stein was shot at his place of business before regular business hours nine days before he was to testify against Branson before a NASSAU County Grand Jury. The assailant was identified as a black male, shot Stein three times.

Stein was offered the federal witness protection program by DEA and the Eastern District of New York, but refused.

It should be noted that during the course of this investigation, in a conversation between Branson and Stein, Branson threatened Stein to the effect that he

(Branson) knew "big guys" and if anyone was fooling around with him, they would be dead.

Subsequently, Branson was convicted in Nassau County District Court of sale of a controlled substance, a Class B felony, and sentenced from 1 1/2 to 4 1/2 years. However, Branson was released earlier and was subsequently seen by Agent Taylor in the vicinity of his residence in Long Beach. it should be noted that Agent Taylor's residence is not near any main thoroughfares, and it is deemed most peculiar that Robert Branson should be seen in that vicinity.

The same evening that Agent Taylor saw Robert Branson outside his residence, two gunman ambushed Stein as he attempted to enter his residence in Dix Hills New York. The gunmen used a shotgun and a 9 mm to kill Stein and his German Shepherd guard dog.

The homicide investigation is being handled by the Suffolk County police department homicide squad.

On a parallel issue, Lorenzo Endario and Jusieppe D'Abrevio were arrested on Title 18 Bribery charges in connection with the bribes taken to secure the aforementioned green cards. They were both sentenced to three years' incarceration with two years *and nine months suspended. 13 aliens were also arrested for being involved in the I-551 stamp impressions game but prosecution with declined in favor of INS administrative action. All were deported to their countries of origin.*

Analysis of Threat Potential against Special Agent Taylor.

The fact that Branson was observed in Agent Taylor's neighborhood and that on the evening that Stein was killed, Taylor received three hang up phone calls is indeed cause for concern. This concern is shared by Suffolk County homicide Detective Mike Davies, who is handling the investigation. Davies stated that Branson is the targets of the investigation and that in his opinion Branson views Taylor as a corrupt federal agent. Davies believes that Stein may have taken additional monies from Branson to allegedly pay to Taylor. This set of circumstances creates additional concerned, since the normal prohibitions against killing law-enforcement officers who are "just doing their job" might not apply. These concerns are also shared by Davies' supervisor Detective Ali McGough.

It was also indicated that a homicide investigation will take a considerable period of time and that no quick arrests are anticipated. As part of the investigation, the Suffolk County Homicide Squad is conducting periodic surveillance at Taylor's residence. At their request, Taylor's government vehicle is parked on a random basis at his residence.

In conclusion, I must concur with the concerns of Suffolk County homicide squad. We have an usual situation where an agent performed in an outstanding matter in a protracted undercover investigation resulting in the possibility of a threat against his life. Given the persistence and patience displayed by the murderers of Stein, it will be almost impossible to provide adequate long-term protection for Agent Taylor, if he is to be assigned within the immediate area. In view of this, I believe serious consideration should be given to reassignment outside the New York area, at least until the homicide investigation is successfully concluded.

Jake, as he completed reading the fax was startled as his phone rang.

District Director Slaughterly's assistant Naveyda was calling to advise him that until a long-term place was found for Jake, he was to be transferred to the Portland Maine office of the FBI under a fictitious name. She asked Jake to suggest a name for himself that he would quickly remember. As he tried to think of a name not associated with his close family and friends, Naveyda blurted out,

"I've got it, how about Tom Jones? He's personally my favorite artist and it's an easy name to remember"

"Special Agent Tom Jones it is then" Jake replied.

Portland, Maine, a beautiful place in the summer is a brutal place in the winter. After an extremely boring two weeks being followed by FBI support personnel all trying to keep warm, Jake heard from Washington that he had been reassigned to the FBI Headquarters in Washington DC and that he would no longer need his "bodyguards".

Relieved he boarded a plane to Washington and moved into a small hotel in Crystal City, Virginia. At first he would travel daily into DC and attend computer educational classes. Once he exhausted the classes, he became a professional tourist. He visited every museum, art event and sports events he could fine. Still bitter after being passed over for the position of Supervisory Special Agent, he decided that he would enjoy himself at the expense of his office.

Unfortunately, he could not pursue his Equal Employment Opportunity claim as he would not be able to be present at the hearings for his own safety.

After two months, Jake had seen enough, done enough and was ready to go home. He rang his office in Manhattan and told them he no longer needed protection and that he would be back at work on Monday. He flew home to New York with bodyguards at his side. One of his bodyguards was Chinese and believed in many superstitions. As they walked to a waiting car at the airport, a seagull pooped on the Chinese bodyguard's head. He immediately started to panic and tell Jake that this was a very bad sign for Jake. Jake told him the exact opposite. He told him this was the greatest of luck and advised him to buy a lottery ticket the same day.

Back at his office, he was somewhat skeptical on what he was coming back to. He did not have to wait long before receiving an order to be seen by Dr. Presso, a psychiatrist who would evaluate his status before being cleared for duty again. Mark Presso was a bespectacled little man, who never looked up from the pad he was writing on. After a time, it was quite clear that Dr Presso had an agenda. His questions, although different, surrounded two topics, depression and anger.

"How could you not be depressed, Jake? The witness you had been working with was shot and now your own life is in jeopardy" Dr Presso suggested.

"Are you not angry that you were passed over for a promotion that you deserved?" and "did you not face charges at one time for exploiting New York State?" Presso demanded.

After he had summated this countless times and in different ways, Jake began to find the whole thing quite comical. The upper echelon had tried to get him terminated by fabricating evidence, now they were trying to have him classed as unfit for duty.

After four sessions, Presso gave up the fight and cleared him to go back to full duty.

Throwing himself back into work, he began work on operations out of JFK airport. Jake was specifically detailed to the Smuggling Unit. The operation, massive in scope, targeted all the International Airports in New York, New Jersey and Washington DC.

As he began to transfer his office over to JFK, he learned of another vacancy for a Supervisory Special Agent. At first, he could not decide whether to apply after the debacle from his last application. This time, however, he would be out of the JFK office on the Smuggling unit. He decided that he had nothing to lose.

He prepared his application and then went to the local stationery store to photocopy all his letters of commendations, awards etc. The weather was brutal, cold, windy and pouring with rain. By the time he got to the stationers, he was drenched. As he began to copy the paperwork, he heard a voice behind him.

"You're Agent Taylor," said a soft feminine voice.

He turned to see a young, tall and very attractive brunette.

"I am" he replied, not sure where this was going.

"You live in Long Beach, not far from where I am in Queens"

"I do" Taylor immediately on guard. Why would she know that?

"I'm Isabel. I work at the Federal Building, in the Clerks' office. I've heard lots about you and I would love to hear more. Would you like to join me for coffee, my treat?"

"I would love to, but my life is crazy right now" Jake replied as he gathered all the paperwork to take to the counter and pay. "Perhaps another time."

He turned to face the counter and dropped his wallet. Isabel immediately bent down, picked it up and handed it to Jake. She turned and walked to the shop door and looked out at the rain, even heavier than before. She turned back to look at Jake.

"Could I get a ride with you Agent Taylor?"

Every piece of Taylor's being told him to decline.

"Of course," he answered. "Are you going home?"

In the car, Isabel brought Jake up to speed on her life, her young daughter and the guy who had left her on finding out she was pregnant. Jake was more reserved and let Isabel do all the talking. She began to question Jake about if he was in a relationship. Jake advised he was, figuring that would be the end of that subject.

Once home, Isabel asked him if he would like to come up to her apartment. He politely declined. He headed home and wrote a mental note to himself to take a framed picture of an old girlfriend to work the following day.

Although about to move offices for the Smuggling unit, Jake put the picture of his former girlfriend on his desk. He left the office to take a few things over to JFK, when he returned the picture had gone. As he sat at his desk, Isabel put her head around the door and reminded him that she still owed him a cup of coffee. Jake decided that he needed to tell her he wasn't interested. He had too much stress in his life already, he didn't need a relationship to make matters worse. He agreed to the coffee, providing it was in the cafeteria on the ninth floor.

They sat at a table near the window. Jake took a deep breath and as kindly as he could, told her that he was in a committed relationship and that they would not be seeing each other again. Isabel looked around in embarrassment to ensure no one was listening to the conversation. She smiled at him as she stood up,

"Your loss Agent Taylor"

He returned to his office and put the rest of his items in a file box. He threw his coat over his shoulders and headed to JFK.

Jake's partner in the Smuggling unit was an old buddy of his, Special Agent Keith Lenney. From a good Irish Catholic family, Keith had married an Irish girl out of Dublin. He was trying to put himself through Law School to provide a better life for them both. Keith had the ability to survive on two hours of sleep, and still look like he had slept all night. He was always upbeat and ready to go.

Jake and Keith would work from 7am until 11pm on many days. He was happy to be busy. He had not been sleeping well due to six or seven calls on his telephone during the night. Each one of them a hang up. He was also getting numerous pages during the day, to the point that his partner commented that he had become a very popular guy. Each page gave him telephone number to call. On every occasion he called, no one answered the number. Jake had the uncanny feeling that the caller was Isabel. Concerned, Jake placed a call to the Manhattan OPR (Office of Professional Responsibility). He spoke to a female agent and filled her in on what was going on. Susan asked Jake if he had any proof. He told her that he didn't but maybe it was nothing. He just wanted to have it documented.

It was during one of these 18-hour days, that Jake received notice that he had not been successful in his application for the Supervisory Special Agent. What was more incredible was that Jake had 17 years' experience and 27 citations for superior and exemplary dedication to the agency. The successful applicant, Fred Applegate, had four years' experience and 4 citations. The injustice was so blatant and so provocative, Jake immediately filed another Equal Employee Opportunity Claim and had no doubt that the decision would be reversed.

Keith began to worry about Jake. He was no longer the upbeat, friendly and talkative buddy that Keith had known over the years. He tried to talk to Jake to no avail.

Intel had come into the JFK office that a flight from Colombia the following day would have two passengers smuggling cocaine. Keith and Jake decided to work undercover and dressed in jeans and sweaters, they mingled in with the crowd departing the Colombian flight and made their way to Baggage Claim.

The flight had been full so there were many passengers milling around the carousel waiting for luggage. The sniffer dogs had not hit on any suitcases prior to them being placed on the carousel. Little by little the cases began to disappear with their owners until two large black duffel bags were left circling the carousel. Keith walked up and down the area with his arms thrown up in the air loudly complaining that his bags were missing. Two young women, also stood waiting. Jake stood back watching the scene. The woman, probably early twenties, looked nervous. They looked around and whispered to each other, then looked around again. Eventually one of the, moved forward, joined by the other and each picked up a matching duffle bag.

Jake walked over to the women as they moved towards the exit. He identified himself and was soon joined by Keith. The women, who spoke little English, were asked to accompany the Agents into the Customs offices. They were sat in an interview room, with a female Customs agent and asked to place their duffel bags on the table.

In the meantime, Jake contacted a Federal Judge, to request a verbal order of authorization to allow Jake and Keith to open the duffel bags. The judge asked what probable cause they had. Jake explained the intel and the circumstances which had occurred in Baggage Claim. The Judge asked Jake if the dogs had hit upon the bags, Jake advised that they had not. The Judge was reluctant to give the order without more information.

"Your Honor, there is something in those bags. I can't explain why the dogs didn't hit on them but every cell in my body tells me that they contain drugs. I've been doing this a long time and I will bet my career on it"

"Agent Taylor, you are asking me, on your hunch, that I give you an order to violate the rights of two foreign individuals on United States soil?" The Judge bellowed down the phone.

"Yes sir that's exactly what I'm asking" Jake replied holding the phone in one hand and his fingers crossed on the other.

A brief silence ensued. Eventually the Judge cleared his throat,

"Ok Agent Taylor, let's hope you are correct. I expect to hear from in in one hour with a positive outcome. If I don't hear from you, I expect you in my chambers tomorrow morning at 8am. Is that clear Special Agent"

"Loud and clear your Honor. I will contact you within the hour"

Jake returned to the interview room and nodded to Keith. He looked at the camera in the corner of the room. The red light was on below it showing it was operational. He asked the female customs officer if she had the passports of the two young women. She passed them to Jake. He read out loud,

"Maria Gonzales-Flores and Helena Gomez. Si? Jake looked at both girls.

Both nodded and looked extremely pale.

"We have reason to believe that you are carrying an illegal substance in your bag. Tenemos motivos para creer que lleva una sustancia illegal en sus maletas."

Neither woman replied but the smaller of the two, Maria Gonzales-Flores began to sob.

"I am an FBI Agent and I am authorized by United States law to search your bags. Soy un agente del FBI y estoy autorizado la ley de los Estados Unidos para registrar sus maletas."

Helena stood up straight and looked forward. Maria held onto her and continued to sob.

Jake and Keith opened a bag each and began to take out the contents and place them on the table. At first, a few items of miscellaneous clothing came out followed by oblong packages which were wrapped in black plastic and taped up with clear tape. Each agent counted 40 packages in each duffel bag.

"What is this? Que es esto?" He lifted one of the packages and looked at Helena.

She shrugged her shoulders.

"No tengo idea? No somos mios"

Jake translated,

" I have no idea? It isn't mine."

Jake put the package down and peeled back some of the tape. Under the black plastic, silver foil could be seen. Jake opened the foil and at the same time, a yellow thick substance started to ooze out. He lifted the package to his nose.

"Well I'll be damned. It's mustard. No wonder the dogs didn't make a hit"

As he peeled away the layers of mustard and foil, a clear plastic revealed a white powder. Jake took a knife and opened the bag. He took a small amount of the powder and placed it into a small vial which the female customs agent handed to him. He shook the vial which promptly turned blue.

"Cocaine. No need for translation". Jake announced. " You are both under arrest. Ambos estan bajo arresto"

He nodded at the Customs officer who placed handcuffs on Helena and escorted out her of the room. Another female customs officer entered and took Maria into a separate room. Jake and Keith labeled and weighed the cocaine which totaled 40 kilos with a street value of over one million US dollars.

Once the cocaine was placed into secured custody, Jake called the Federal Judge and told him of the success.

"That's very good for you Agent Taylor. You see I am not in my chambers tomorrow so you would have had a long wait. Congratulations". The Judge hung up not waiting for a response from Jake.

Jake decided that he would interview Maria and that Keith would get the stoic Helena.

Jake entered the interview room where the female Customs officer was sat at one side of a table with a large tape recorder off to one side. The camera was operational in the far corner of the room. Jake sat down opposite Maria. He knew straight away she would talk, either that or she would vomit.

Immediately she began to talk, in between sobs. Jake found it hard to keep up with her as she spoke quickly in Spanish. It seems her father had got into trouble with a cartel leader in Cartagena. Maria and Helena (Maria's cousin) had agreed to carry the duffel bags to the United States to save her father's life. They did not know what was in the bags as they had not opened them. The clothes which were also in the bags did not belong to them either. She became very distraught as she told Jake that her father would now die.

Jake left the room and joined Keith. He was getting nowhere with Helena and an interpreter. Jake told Keith in front of Helena what had transpired with Maria.

Helena broke her silence,

"This is not the real, no it is not the real, it is falsa, falsa. Ellas no son nuestras bolsas, not bags no belong us"

Jake answered,

 "Ok so why did you pick up the bags? Por que recogiste las melatas?"

"No lo se. I do not know this" Helena answered "I say no more, no mas".

Jake told the Customs officer officer to process both women and have them arraigned.

Jake and Keith returned to their office and began writing reports. Jake's phone rang,

 "Taylor, it's Agent Valerio. I understand you just made arrests for forty keys of Coke"

Jake rolled his eyes,

"Yes that is correct".

"Agent Taylor, what are you wearing?"

"Excuse me" Jake retorted.

"Did you not understand the question Taylor, what are you wearing?"

"I am wearing a blue suit, white shirt and grey tie" as he looked down at his blue jeans and cream sweater.

"Taylor. You and your partner are to report immediately to Federal Plaza and report to Bob Slaughterly's office, immediately"

Click the phone went dead.

"Thank you, Agent Valerio. Yes Agent Valerio it was quite a collar. Yes, over a million dollars of Coke. No really, congratulations, thats a little too much, it's what I'm paid to do" he mockingly shouted down the phone before slamming it onto the receiver.

"Hey Keith" he shouted through to the office next door. "Grab your coat. I hope you have a suit in your car. We're going to Manhattan to see Slaughterly and my best friend Valerio"

Keith walked into Jake's office.

"What?"

"Well it seems that Valerio has his own little spies here. Not only did he hear of our collar, he also knows what we are wearing".

"No sorry, still not following" Keith questioned.

"Do you have a suit in your car?" Jake demanded.

"Yes" Keith replied.

"Then get it and meet me at my car. Don't forget dress shoes. We are going to Manhattan. I'll fill you in on the way".

Jake grabbed his jacket and car keys and made his way out of the office walked toward parking lot.

He turned around to see if Keith was following him. No sign of him yet. Jake continued towards his car muttering under his breath. He was about to put his key in the lock, when he heard a noise behind him. He turned suddenly and saw a young Hispanic man, no more than twenty years old. He had a pistol and was aiming it at Jake.

"Whoa man. What the hell" Jake exclaimed loudly.

"This is from a good friend of yours, remember Bob?"

Jake hurled his car keys at the shooter which deflected the gun. The shot rang out but hit the ground. The shooter took off running toward the chainlink fence which surrounded the parking lot. He was much taller and agile than Jake, he took a running jump almost clearing the fence, pushed off the top of the fence and landed on the other side.

Jake could hear Keith behind him yelling. Jake also took a running jump but wasn't quite as lucky as the shooter. He caught his right foot at the edge of the fence and landed heavily on the ground.

The shooter was well away by the time Jake got up and limped painfully back to the car. Keith met him, sweating and panting, his runner also absconded. Jake removed his shoe to reveal a very obvious fracture to his right great toe.

Chapter Nine

The foot surgeon, Dr Schofield, was pleased on how the surgery had gone. He told Mrs. Taylor, Jake's Mom, that this was the first time he'd worked on a toe broken in a criminal pursuit. Jake rolled his eyes as she listed all the other ailments Jake had suffered as an FBI agent. Then she launched into childhood injuries, at the same time Dr Schofield edged his way backwards out of the room.

"So it's settled. You can spend the first week with me" Jake's Mom stated with a grin on her face.

"No it's not settled. I said I would stay with you for a couple of days until I'm on my feet again and able to walk in that boot contraption". He had a "not fit for duty note" for a month as the doctor wanted limited weight bearing for the fracture and tendons to heal. Jake had argued this, but the doctor remained insistent.

For the next four weeks, Jake caught up with friends and family and forgot about work. The accident had come at a good time for him. He was able to escape the nightmare he was living at work. When it came time to return, Jake seriously considered not going back. All it took was Keith asking him whether he was going to let the bastards win.

He returned to the Federal Building to drop off paperwork stating he was fit for light duty. He was taken aback when Agent Valerio met him at the door to his office and told him to report to the Director Slaughterly's office.

"Please sit-down Agent Taylor" Slaughterly announced as Jake walked in.

"Sexual harassment is a huge issue in the workplace today, Agent Taylor. I would like you to report to JFK airport to meet with a team from Washington to talk about this subject"

"What now?" Taylor answered finding the whole situation quite odd.

"Yes. Meet in Conference Room B12 in the Customs building. You should be there by 10:30am"

Jake raced across town and picked up the subway direct line to JFK. Arriving twenty minutes early, he located the conference room, grabbed a Coke and waited for everyone else to arrive.

At 10:30, two men in dark suits came in the room and introduced themselves as OPR agents (Office of Professional Responsibility) from the Washington DC office. It became quite obvious to Jake that no one else was invited to this session.

"My name is Agent John Roberts and this is Agent Jerry McDaniels. We have received a disturbing complaint of sexual harassment against you Agent Taylor"

Jake sat back in his seat. He knew exactly what was going on. He reached down into his briefcase and pulled out a small tape recorder. He switched it to record and waited for the agents to continue.

"Agent Taylor, you are not permitted to record this interview"

"I don't believe I am under arrest" Jake replied. "I am prepared to continue with this interview, however I will be taping it. Take it or leave it gentlemen" Jake stood up as if to leave.

Agent Roberts told him to sit down and leave the tape recording.

"Did you, Agent Taylor, in a government vehicle, drive Ms Isabel Rosen to her home at approximately 5:30pm on October 21st of this year?"

"Yes I did" Jake replied.

"Can you tell us what happened when you arrived at her apartment?" Roberts continued.

"When I arrived at her apartment building, Ms. Rosen invited me to come up to her apartment. I declined and drove myself home"

"Agent Taylor, Ms. Rosen has told us that you were the one who invited yourself up to her apartment and that you tried to sexually assault her"

"That is categorically untrue" Jake calmly replied.

"Do you also deny stalking Ms. Rosen, going back to her apartment and calling her during the night?"

"Yes I do deny this" Jake replied. "Can you advise me what proof you have to warrant this allegation?"

"We are in the initial stages of this investigation. Agent Valerio referred the case to Washington due to the seriousness of the allegations".

"I bet he did" Jake retorted. "I would strongly suggest that you check the history on Ms. Rosen's home phone and office phone before we move any further with this interview. If you want to continue with this allegation once you have done this, please contact my attorney, Roger Aparrone. I have a strong feeling that you won't find this necessary. Good day gentlemen"

Jake flipped of the recorder, placed it in his briefcase and walked out of the room.

Although portraying a strong and defiant stance, Jake was anything but. He felt sick to stomach and devastated. The consequences of these actions could have ended his career as well as his freedom. Thank God he had contacted OPR with his concerns that Isabel was stalking him. This had been documented and would also prove his innocence. He truly believed that Valerio was behind this. He knew Valerio hated him, but this was a very low blow even for him. He called Roger when he arrived home and confided his fears to him.

"I'm frightened Roger. I have never been this scared of anything or anyone before"

"Stay strong."

Back at the Federal Building, he once again was met by Valerio.

"Your doctor has stated that you are to return to light duty at this time. Director Slaughterly and I would like to meet with you. We have a special assignment in mind which will meet your light duty requirements. You can leave for the day and we will meet you in the conference room at 8am tomorrow morning.

Jake walked into conference room, Tuesday morning at precisely 7.55am. Director Slaughterly was sat at the conference table conversing with a young lady sat in front of a typewriter. Agent Valerio was on the telephone holding a large mug of coffee. When he saw Jake walk into the room, he ended his conversation and beckoned for Jake to sit.

"Agent Taylor due to your current condition we find it necessary to cancel your detail to JFK airport. Your new position will be working in the Criminal Aliens

Section under the supervision of Fred Applegate. Also, you will not be given a government car, nor are you sanctioned to ride in one".

"You have got to be kidding! First of all, I trained Fred Applegate and have 15 years more experience and I'd like you to explain why I cannot ride in a government car. How does my light duty status cause me not to be allowed to sit in a moving vehicle"

"That's the rules Son" Slaughterly chipped in.

"Sir, please do not call me Son, we are approximately the same age"

He turned to the lady typing in the corner.

"Ma'am please document that I, Agent Jake Taylor, believe that these actions are retaliatory and pure harassment. I believe that Director Slaughterly and Agent Valerio are punishing me for filing an Equal Employment Opportunity case against the department. This adverse transfer is disciplinary and illegal."

The lady nodded at him as she continued to type.

"Take it or leave it Taylor. That's the order. If you choose not to comply then you will be terminated"

"Oh I will comply" scoffed Jake. "You will never get me to quit, no matter what you do to me"

Valerio turned to the typist, asked her to stop writing.

"Taylor, if it's the last thing I do on this earth, it will be to fire you. You are to report to Supervisor Applegate immediately"

With that Slaughterly and Valerio left the room.

"Ma'am could you make sure I get a copy of what just transpired".

The lady began to stutter a reply and then stopped,

"Absolutely Sir" she smiled at Jake and winked her eye.

Supervisor Applegate was sat at his desk when Jake entered his office.

"Agent Taylor. This is somewhat awkward for both of us. I expect you to act professionally and follow my orders. You will need to take public transportation to the office. In other words, you cannot hitch a ride with other agents"

"Don't you find that a little odd Fred"

"My name is Supervisor Applegate. Please address me as such"

Jake was at the end of his tether.

"You are going to fucking act this way with me after all I did for you. You ate at my home, I worked around your family issues, I basically made you what you are today."

"Agent Taylor, you are formally suspended for three days, without pay, for serious misconduct. Please leave immediately"

Jake stormed out of the room, grabbed his coat and left the building.

He immediately contacted his attorney Roger Aparrone. Roger was as flabbergasted as Jake. He told Jake to go home and he would think about what to do next. Never in his thirty years of practice had he ever come across such blatant misdoings in a government agency. He would really have to think things through.

Jake also contacted the Equal Employment Opportunity Commission and left a message for the Commissioner to call him. The telephone operator asked if he wanted to leave a message. Jake replied:

"You simply do not have enough paper"

Roger's first advice to Jake was to return to work and just do his job. Document everything and do everything they tell you.

He returned to work, by train, on Friday morning and was told to report to Doctor Presso, the Government Psychologist. Per Roger's advice, he took the three flights of stairs to Dr. Presso's office.

"Welcome back, Agent Taylor. I believe we have some subjects to discuss. I have been told by your supervisor that you threatened him this past Monday".

"That is absolutely not true" Jake recounted what had taken place between Fred Applegate and himself. He explained what had transpired since his accident and even referred to some of the treatment he had suffered prior.

Dr. Presso did not look up. He just stared at his pad and seemed to write far more that what Jake was telling him. Eventually, he looked up and told Jake he would need to surrender his government revolver.

"No problem" Jake answered "I'm getting good at that"

Dr. Presso advised Jake that he was to return to his office Monday morning at 9am, until then he was free to leave for the day.

Jake remained seated:

"Am I on the payroll again?"

Dr. Presso confirmed this and asked Jake to leave.

It was his sister's birthday so he decided to surprise her on his way home. Kate had taken the day off from her job so they decided pick up their mother and go out for lunch. Jake was careful not to tell either of them what was happening at work. He told them that he'd decided to take the day off and visit them both. After a bottle of wine, Jake took his mother home tipsy. He drove his sister's car chatting the whole time to his family on the back seat. They seemed not to be interested in what he had to say. At the traffic light, he looked over his shoulder to see Kate and his Mother fast asleep leaning on each other.

"Light weights" he uttered under his breath.

Monday morning and Jake was right on time in Dr. Presso's office at 9am. Jake sat down on the sofa outsider the Dr's room. Fred Applegate walked into the office and told Jake to take a seat at the desk.

"Agent Taylor, I need to make you aware that you are the subject of a Tarasoff Warning"

"A what?" Jake loudly remarked.

"A Tarasoff warning is when a therapist has the duty to warn appropriate persons that a patient may present a risk of harm to a specific person or persons".

"I know what a Tarasoff warning is, Fred. How can they possibly label me with that"?

"Dr Presso has deemed you a danger to other agency employees whom you have had a history of conflict with. He has called you quarrelsome and easily agitated. It is the duty of Dr Presso to determine if you pose a serious danger of violence. In his professional opinion you meet this criterion therefore he must act to protect the victim(s). As a result of this decision, you may no longer work with supervisors with whom you have had conflict in the past. Since Agent Valerio is one of those supervisors and is also the indirect supervisor of every Special Agent in the Investigations Branch, at this time you are being placed under paid Administration Leave. As this is paid leave, you are obligated to call, by telephone, the office every working day. You may not take other employment at this time as this will lead to immediate termination. Do you understand Agent Taylor?".

Jake was dumbfounded.

"Do you understand Agent Taylor?"

Jake stood up, nodded his head and began to walk out the door.

"Before you leave, I need your credentials"

Jake replied "I do not have them with me; you will have to collect them from my home"

"I will send you home in a government car with another agent. You will give the agent your credentials when you arrive"

"Sorry, I cannot do that Sir" Jake retorted. "I'm not allowed to ride in a government car"

Jake walked out of the office and out of the building. He would not return for another 18 months. During that time, the tax payer paid Jake's salary and in return, got nothing! Ironically, for 18 months, the Government cost the tax payers thousands of dollars for a crime which Jake would be ultimately exonerated. This, in itself, was more of a crime than anything Jake had been accused of. If indeed Jake had been "double dipping" with the City of Long Beach and the FBI, the amount stolen would have been far less than the amount of money used to pay Jake on suspension for 18 months.

During this time, Jake reached out to his senators and congressmen. He wrote to the upper echelon of the Justice Department; in fact he wrote to anyone and everyone he thought may be able to help. He received many promises, all turned out to be empty.

He also travelled to Costa Rica with a friend to go white water rafting. Deep in the rainforest he made his daily call to the office, as instructed. His call was always answered by Susan Mitchell, one of the management team in the Personnel office. Susan and Jake had become friendly over the months. This time Susan asked him where he was calling from as she could hear water dripping in the background. He wanted to tell her that he was in the Amazon rainforest but told her that his shower was running in the background.

Roger Aparrone and Jake had decided that they would not file any lawsuits until Jake retired. The maximum retirement age for the Justice Department was 57. The minimum age 50. At the time Jake was put on administrative leave, he was 48. He fully intended to work to age 57. He knew that he could not file a suit until the agency could not hurt him anymore. He would document everything giving him the satisfaction that when he did sue, he would have everything he needed.

During the 18 months of leave, Jake was seen by the workplace psychiatrist Ian McDonald who he had worked with, some years back, during the allegations of him working at two jobs concurrently. Dr Ian McDonald wrote to the District Director Bob Slaughterly stating that Dr Presso had told him that he was not allowed to talk in detail about the case, and that he had been resistant in answering certain questions. Dr. McDonald had reached out to the Medical Board which advised Dr. Presso of his legal obligation to answer the questions of a participating Psychiatrist.

His letter to Director Slaughterly included,

"It is my opinion, based on Dr Presso's lack of cooperation with this evaluation, that his Tarasoff Warning does not appear credible and germane to Agent Taylor's current functioning. Of particular significance, is that Agent Taylor never made any specific threats towards any individual nor did he articulate any plan to carry out any harm against any individual. This information was verified by Dr Presso.

Consistent with this assessment, Taylor stated that the Tarasoff warning was not the result of any threat he posed, but rather the result of pressure placed on Presso by the FBI which caused Presso to compromise his professional integrity and declare Taylor to be a threat. Taylor stated that Presso acknowledged to Taylor that he knew the FBI was "after" Taylor and that the FBI would "go to great lengths" to "get" him. Taylor also stated that Presso had told him that he had never seen so much FBI paperwork about one individual, and stated "If I could, I would like to see you in a one-man office out of Montauk Point looking for German submarines". Taylor stated that he interpreted this statement as indicating that Taylor was in some danger.

These statements make reasonable argument for the reasons that Taylor has been placed on administrative leave".

Within two weeks of Dr. Ian McDonald writing this letter, Jake received a letter from the US Department of Justice. The letter was dated 13 days prior to his 50th birthday.

"Dear Mr. Taylor,

This is to advise you that as of this coming January 2nd, your administrative leave is terminated. On that date you are to return to full duty. Furthermore, you are hereby reassigned to the position of a Deportation Officer effective upon your return to duty. You are to report at 8am to the Supervisory Detention and Deportation Office at the Service Processing Center in New York.

Eric McMullen

District Director

This reassignment was effectively a demotion. Agent Taylor knew he had them! He just had to return to work and he could prove discrimination, retaliation and harassment. He also knew that he had to have a second surgery on his toe injured in the pursuit of a shooter. He decided to return for two weeks, have the surgery, fulfill the sick leave, then retire. He advised Roger of his plan, who agreed wholeheartedly.

Three days following his 50th birthday, Jake presented himself at the Deportation Service Office and introduced himself to the Supervisor. She had absolutely no idea who he was and why he had been transferred to her office. Jake sat at her desk while she called the Personnel Management Supervisor. Jake heard the person on the line say,

"You mean he really showed up"?

His new supervisor sent him over to Personnel to pick up his transfer papers. He was given a wad of papers held together with a paper clip. On his way back to Deportation he read the papers. On one, it was typed in upper case letters "NO PROMOTION POTENTIAL"

He slipped into the adjoining office to his new supervisor and copied the papers before giving them to her.

For the two weeks he worked, he was not given a badge or credentials, nor a computer password, nor a computer, in fact, not even a desk or workspace. He documented everything and took photos when he was able.

He left the agency for the last time to have surgery on his great toe again. He remained on sick leave for six weeks, at which point he retired.

This complaint was heard at the United States District Court for the Southern District of New York.

Plaintiff Jake Taylor began work for the FBI in 1976 at age 30. On two occasions during the plaintiff's career, the FBI published a vacancy for a Supervisory Criminal Investigator. On each occasion the plaintiff was not selected for the job. In response to his non selection, Taylor filed two Equal Employment Opportunity complaints stating that the decision not to promote him on both occasions was discriminatory based on the experience and qualification of the successful applicants. The plaintiff testified that he was told by Agent Valerio that the agents selected were considered superior, and the plaintiff, quarrelsome and unexemplary. The plaintiff disputes this stating that he has received numerous awards and written commendations for his outstanding interpersonal skills. On three occasions when he was to be awarded a QSI (Quality Step Increase), approved by two supervisors, Agent Valerio denied it. At the same time, Valerio approved every QSI for Taylor's colleagues.

The plaintiff also testified that on two occasions, he was ordered not to drive or even ride in a government car and his use of a government firearm suspended. The plaintiff claimed he was subject to a hostile work environment where non promotion decisions were retaliatory for his EEO activity. He claimed he was subjected to disparate treatment, retaliation, and a constructive discharge in violation of Title VII of the Employment Act.

Following a work-related injury which caused the need for surgery on the Plaintiff's foot, he was transferred, in a retaliatory move, to a lesser position supervised by a protégé trained by the plaintiff. This was one of the occasions when he was told he could no longer drive nor ride in a government car. The other occasion was when he was treated in the hospital for a Mitral Valve Prolapse. The plaintiff alleges acts of abuse from supervisors and provided evidence from workers stating that they were told not to speak to the plaintiff, that he was "nuts", having a nervous breakdown, suffered from "emotional problems" and had made 149 threats against FBI employees. They also stated that Supervisor Applegate broke into Taylor's desk and purposefully discarded some of Taylor's personal belongings in order to harass him.

Another coworker provided an affidavit stating that FBI supervisors purposefully harassed Taylor and made his work environment unusually and unnecessarily unpleasant on a nearly daily basis. The actions of Supervisor Applegate took against Mr. Taylor on a daily basis led her to conclude that Applegate lived to make Jake Taylor's life on hell on earth. She was told not to speak to Mr. Taylor and often witnessed Applegate with other supervisors standing around his desk, on one occasion Applegate had his forefinger pointing in Jake Taylor's face, standing at his desk, yelling at him.

The plaintiff also states that the FBI service placed him on administrative leave based on a psychologist Tarasoff Warning. The warning stated that he posed danger to other agency employees with whom he had a history of conflict. The plaintiff claims the real reason for the administrative leave was because of protected EEO activity, retaliation and a non credible Tarasoff Warning which also breached his right to confidentiality.

The plaintiff also claims that his transfer to the Deportation Service following his administrative leave was unlawful and that he was not furnished with the tools needed to complete this task i.e. a firearm, badge, desk resulting in an adverse work environmental causing the Plaintiff to retire seven years early.

It took over two months to get a decision. When it came, it was devastating for Jake.

The United States Court for the Southern District of New York granted the DEFENDANTS motion for summary judgement on ALL claims and dismissed the PLAINTIFFS complaints. In granting the summary judgement, the district court found Taylor had not demonstrated a case of discrimination in the failure to promote him, nor had he provided evidence of a hostile work environment. His claim of retaliation from the EEO claims was denied together with his forced departure from employment. Finally, the District Court denied the plaintiffs demand for punitive damages and attributed "the incidents the plaintiff describe appear to be attributable to personal animosity".

Jake was devastated. He could not fathom how they felt that the emotional pain he had suffered for so many years', was attributed to his own actions. For the first time in his life he was truly frightened. He felt abandoned and very alone.

Roger Aparrone tried to reach him but Jake did not want to talk. He stayed indoors in his condo and became reclusive and depressed.

About two weeks after the decision, he awoke at 10am with a pounding headache having drank heavily the night before. Under his door was a note.

"The only thing necessary for the triumph of evil is that good men do nothing"
Call me.
Roger.

The appeal was heard exactly 21 months after the case had been dismissed in its entirety by the District Court. It was heard by the United States Court of Appeals, Second Circuit.

Jake Taylor, Plaintiff-Appellant

  V

John Ashcroft Attorney General

Robert Slaughterly, Individually and in his official capacity.

David Valerio, Individually and in his official capacity

Fred Applegate, Individually and in his official capacity

Defendants- Appellees

Excruciatingly it took another 18 months for a decision to be rendered by the Court. To overturn the decision from the District Court was going to be almost impossible; it seemed that was the case as month after month passed.

Jake, in the interim, had gone back to the beach to Lifeguard in the summer. Since he had missed a year (caused by the FBI denying his request), Jake had to retake the grueling lifeguard test. At 50 years old, he repeated the test he had taken at age 15. He swam 100 yards in one minute and then another 25 yards, rescued a fighting victim, held the victim in a cross-chest hold, then swam another 25 yards. This was done at an indoor pool. The next test was a three quarter of a mile run in soft sand on the beach in under six minutes, then a run, swim, run course involving a 500-yard swim, in May, in freezing open water. The stroke could not be broken and stopping was an immediate disqualification. It was tough but Jake did it with time to spare, embarrassing new lifeguards half his age by beating every one of them.

He had also taken a position of Dean of Discipline at a local high school. He monitored all the detentions, chaperoned on every field trip and made himself available for tutoring. He did everything to take his mind off the court case. Although busy with his new career, he felt that his life was on hold.

Roger Aparrone was the first to receive the decision of the Appellate Court. He called Jake immediately and arranged a lunchtime meeting. As he waited for Jake to arrive, he quickly scanned the twenty-four-page document and re read it another two times. Each plaintiff complaint was addressed individually and compared with similar cases of precedent.

Jake arrived at Roger's office building, deep in Manhattan. His secretary led him into the cozy office.

Nervously he questioned Roger

"Do I want to know?"

Roger replied:

"Do you want to read it?"

"Hell no I can't read it. Tell me what it says"

"I will read the conclusion of the Court" he flicked to the final page of the document.

"For the reasons stated in this case, we VACATE the districts court's grant of summary judgment on Taylor's claim which is based on discrimination, and find that Taylor proved his allegations of discrimination, retaliation and the failure to promote him. He also provided evidence of a hostile work environment and punitive actions based on two EEO complains causing a forced departure from employment. We AFFIRM the district court's decision as to the availability of punitive damages under Title VII however notwithstanding, we award damages costs on appeal to the plaintiff-appellant at the highest rate available under said Title.

End of document"

"You won man. You just overturned the ruling of United States District Court for the Southern District of New York. Shit, I have never actually seen that happen before. You just made history".

Addendum

Jake Taylor, his wife Karen (a former nurse) and Yorkshire Terrier, Chester live in a beautiful waterfront home in Sarasota County, Florida. Both now retired, they enjoy a happy life. Jake continues to swim daily in his lap pool and could still pass the lifeguard test, although chooses not to. They enjoy traveling the World, taking road trips across America and boating in the Sarasota waters. Jake, his wife and Chester, a certified therapy dog, volunteer for a non profit hospice visiting Veterans and patients. They also monetarily assist in many charitable organizations. Therefore endorsing the statement:

"The best revenge is massive success" Frank
Sinatra.

David Valerio, was demoted and ostracized by the District and transferred to a shoe box office at one of the New York Airports. His wife divorced him and his friends abandoned him. He also took action against the FBI for discrimination. He failed on all three occasions. He began his own investigation company which also failed.

William Canery retired as Assistant Director of Investigations. He met Jake, after he had retired, at a social event they both attended. The first words out of Canery's mouth as they shook hands "You got fucked!"

Robert Slaughterly is also still working. He works for a private company calling themselves specialists in immigration and emigration. Slaughterly himself was under investigation and accused of cronyism. He was accused of improper associations with targets, receiving bribes and promoting a protege whom he later married. He was accused by the INS commissioner for low morale in his agency causing many Agents to transfer to other agencies. He was also accused of lack of communication between field officers and the Commissioner located in Washington DC. Most complaints would not leave Slaughterly's desk. Many directors criticized how he did business and no longer wanted to work with him. Slaughterly left the agency in 1998 but the controversy did not end there.

Slaughterly's wife, had dated many of the agents in the New York office (including Jake) prior to hooking up with Slaughterly. She had used some of these past relationships to move up the chain of command, now, as the wife of the District Director nothing, or nobody was going to stop her. After blatantly abusing her position within the New York office, she promoted herself to, of all things, an ethics instructor within the agency. Within months of obtaining this new position, she was arrested and charged with fraud by obtaining money through a scheme where she purchased expensive items and returned substitute items of lesser value to collect the refund of the higher price. This time, Slaughterly could not protect her. The agency first suspended and then removed her from service. On appeal, she was reinstated to a lesser position for one year after which she could apply for any vacant positions. After the year expired, she made countless applications for new positions in law enforcement in the Agency. She was not selected for any of them. She subsequently sued the Department of Justice to Court claiming that the agency had violated their settlement. She was unsuccessful.

Special Agents Jake, Keith, Rick and Scott remain steadfast friends to date. Jake maintains that without these friendships, he would not have survived the Department of Justice.

This book is dedicated to all those who suffer at the hands of bullies in the workplace.

Printed in Great Britain
by Amazon

21172752R00163